PRINCESS AT HELL'S RIFT

J. M. CORNISH

To martin
from
Jack

ISBN: 978-1911477297

A CIP catalogue record for this title is available from the British
Library.

Lemuria

I know most people think princesses are charmed people - with a life full of parties and coronations but I'm about to reveal a more sinister side of their lives which maybe you didn't expect.

This is the story of Princess Madelyn - the most battle hardened princess who ever lived.

Our story starts in the city of Lemuria in the early 1400s. To someone looking at this city from the outside it would appear to be absolutely beautiful and tranquil but it isn't. The King, whose name was Cameron, was a megalomaniac and the most tyrannical person you could ever fear to meet. He thought putting people to death was the answer to his never-ending problems but his daughter knew different - she saw a different solution to the issue, and unlike her father she thought kindness was the resolution. She was about to commence her first battle with her father.

Up in her private quarters on the third floor of the castle Princess Madelyn sat in front of the mirror combing her long scarlet hair, when one of her servants entered the room. "Your highness, the King requests your presence in the throne room immediately," he said.

"Oh great, who is father going to kill today?" said Madelyn sarcastically.

"I don't think there are any executions scheduled for today," said her servant.

"Well that's alright then," said Madelyn getting up and walking over to the door. And upon reaching it she said to her servant, "Take the rest of the day off, go home to your family."

"Thank you your highness," said the servant taking a bow.

"Please," she implored, "Call me Madelyn."

"Yes your highn... Madelyn," said the servant seeing the look on Madelyn's face. Madelyn walked down the corridor, her dress trailing behind her on the hard stone floor. She had hoped that when she had become the crowned Princess of Lemuria that she would have been able to make more decisions but she still had no input in what her father had to say. She stopped at the double brass doors that adorned the throne room. The two towering guards who stood still on either side of the double doors bowed to her before letting her pass. Madelyn walked into the wide room and her eyes immediately set on her father who was sat on a sparkly gold throne at the other end and those green eyes seemed to be looking right through her. The King had short blond hair and had a cloak attached to his armour which he seemed to wear everywhere he went. His crown sat on his head and the ruby that was built into it was sparkling in the light. "Ah you're there," said King Cameron rising from his throne, before walking towards Madelyn, who greeted her father with a kiss on the cheek. Cameron said, "I summoned you here because I wanted to tell you that we will be having a guest joining us this evening."

"Oh really?" said Madelyn, her eyes widening at the thought of having a guest, "Who?"

"Sir William of Greenmont is joining us for a feast tonight in the Royal Dining Quarters," said King Cameron. "Following that we have a few constitutional matters to discuss which means you need to retire to your quarters and not disturb us."

"I shall father," said Madelyn feeling frustrated as she briskly walked out of the throne room. She felt like going down to the market to see if she could get away from it all, her father and his Kingly matters were just so annoying sometimes. She made her way out into one of the many castle courtyards. In the centre lay the well which was the main place to gather water. The walls of the castle were crumbling to pieces already, even though it had been built only a century ago. Madelyn assumed it had something to do with the War of the Slaves, a furious battle, which had occurred between the army of her father and their most fearsome enemy Galidion. Many great men had lost their lives that day and Madelyn hadn't seen Cameron shed a single tear for any of them. She went down into the market, when suddenly out of the corner of her eye, she saw a man slip his hand into a women's pocket and take out a couple of shiny silver coins. The women felt a movement in her pocket and turned around swiftly to see an old man backing away cautiously. Without hesitation the woman screamed, "Guards!" The guards came rushing over. They grabbed the man and forced him onto his knees causing him to drop the coins. Madelyn watched as they clattered against the pavement. "Please," the man begged, "I need the money to feed my children." Madelyn, feeling sorry for the man, gestured to the guards to release him. The guards looked hesitant but they did as she had asked.

"Poor soul," sighed Madelyn looking at the floor before moving on.

"Oh hello," said Madelyn's friend Violet, coming over towards her, "How are you?"

"I'm fine," said Madelyn, turning around to face Violet.

"You don't look it," observed Violet. "Forgive me Madelyn, but you look so sad."

"It's just father," said Madelyn letting out a long sigh, "It's never about anything but kingly business. He never talks to me unless it's about peace treaties and all other unnecessary business."

"I see what you mean," said Violet sympathetically, "But you see, that is just the curse of being a King."

"Then that makes me wish he wasn't," Madelyn whispered to herself.

Sir William of Greenmont

Madelyn watched the large drops of rain as they bounced against her bedroom window. Through the blur she observed a man on horseback making his way towards the castle and Madelyn could just make out the sight of something gold glistening on his head. 'That must be Sir William' thought Madelyn. She looked around at her peaceful quarters and wondered if she should miss the feast and stay where she was but she didn't want to upset her father. She took one glance at herself in the mirror to make sure there weren't any creases in her dress and no tangles in her hair. When she was satisfied that she looked presentable she started to make her way down to the feast. She heard excited chatter as she walked down the many corridors of the castle of Lemuria. She reached the Royal Dining Quarters and saw her father talking to the man she had seen on the horse. Her father saw her and beckoned for her to come over. "Madelyn," said her father when she arrived by his side, "This is Sir William of Greenmont."

"Pleasure to meet you Madam," said William leaning over and kissing Madelyn's hand gently. "The feast is about to start," said Cameron leading Madelyn and William to their seats at the head table. William was sat on the right side of Cameron and Madelyn was sat on the left. Everyone else in the room just chose a seat and then sat down. When everyone was seated King Cameron rose to give a speech. "Thank you all for gathering here today," said Cameron, his mellow tones echoing around the room. "Today marks the start of a new era, the beginning of peace between two cities. Those cities are that of Lemuria and Greenmont. So, I propose a toast to a new and everlasting friendship."

The words, "A new and everlasting friendship," echoed around the room and it seemed to go on for an eternity or at least it seemed so to Madelyn. She had never been to feasts.   She preferred to be sitting around a little table and having a quiet meal, but when you were a princess like Madelyn there was next to no chance of a quiet meal. Her father and her were either having a row about the way to run the city or they had a major accomplishment to celebrate in which case they had feasts like this one. Cameron sat down to the round of the applause for his captivating speech. "Well done," said William patting Cameron on the shoulder, "That was a brilliant speech."

"Thanks," said Cameron clanging his cup of red wine against William's and a few splashes fell out of the cups. Then a dozen waiters came to the head table with plates full of delicious food which included turkey and sausages. There were also fresh vegetables and bread and lots of wine. One of the waiters came over and placed a huge turkey breast smothered in gravy in front of Madelyn and she stared at it hungrily. She may not like feasts but she had to say that the food offered looked delicious.

The feast went on for about five hours, which in Madelyn's opinion was a bit too long. But finally, the feast was over and Madelyn retired to her quarters. She was sat in her bed robes when she heard voices gradually getting louder as they walked down the corridor that was outside her room. "I know we may be signing a peace treaty but that doesn't mean you can break my rules," said a voice that sounded like her father's. "I know," said a voice that had to be William's, "So what are your rules?"

"Oh, there is only one," said King Cameron. "I saw the way you kissed my daughter on the hand earlier and the way you stared at her all through the night. I am not happy. So if you touch my daughter again I will have you burnt at the stake."

"Come, come, I was only saying 'Hello'," protested William.

"Don't argue with me, I forbid it, you must abide by my rules or suffer the consequences," snapped Cameron. Madelyn strained to hear the rest of the conversation but the voices became fainter before finally disappearing down the corridor. Madelyn lent her back against the door and slid slowly to the floor.

The Quietness of the Night

That night Madelyn struggled to get to sleep, the peace treaty was to be signed tomorrow and Greenmont and Lemuria would soon be friends but something was wrong. Madelyn threw her blankets off her and put her dressing gown on. Madelyn crept out of her room, trying her best to be quiet so she wouldn't disturb anyone and have them ask what she was doing up this late at night. The princess made her way down to the ground floor of the castle and strode through the double brass door that were the entrance to the castle. She was now out in the castle courtyard. That was half of her mission; she had escaped the castle without being detected and now she had to find William's servant. The first place she thought of looking was the stables in hope of finding William's servant tending to his master's horse. That was exactly where she found him, at the far end of the stable stroking the horse's muzzle. Madelyn waited till he took a step back from the horse before emerging from the shadows. "Hello," said Madelyn kindly. The servant turned around startled by Madelyn's sudden appearance and stuttered, "P-P-P-Princess Madelyn."

"Yes that's me," said Madelyn walking up and stroking Williams's horse.

"But I thought Cameron didn't let you out of the castle at night because it was too dangerous," said the servant.

"Oh he doesn't," said Madelyn with a great big smirk on her face, "No one knows I'm here, this is just between you and me."

"But what would you want to talk to a pathetic servant like me for?" he said turning back to the horse. "Oh, this and that," said Madelyn removing her hand from the horse's head, "Tell me about William."

"What is there to tell," said the servant shrugging his shoulders.

"Well, let's start with his personality. What is he like?" asked Madelyn.

"Just like any old King to be honest, always busy, always caught up in his constitutional matters."

"Sounds just like my father," said Madelyn with understanding.

"Why are you so interested though?" snapped the servant, "What has anything that my master does have to do with you?"

"Okay then," said Madelyn with a big sigh, "I wanted to build up to it but has William ever had the desire to steal the throne."

"No," said the servant with a look that said he was hiding something, "Why would you say that?"

"Look," said Madelyn grabbing his arm and looking into his eyes with a scared expression "I think he means to kill my father." The servant broke away from her grasp and looked down at the straw on the floor with a sad expression. "Please," said Madelyn, "Tell me if he has tried to do this before."

The servant gave in and said, "There was one time."

"Go on," said Madelyn encouragingly.

"He tried to steal a throne during the confusion of the War of the Slaves," replied the servant.

"Whose?" asked Madelyn.

"King Leo," relied the servant.

"He must be insane," exclaimed Madelyn, "King Leo is one of the most dangerous kings Hell's Rift has ever known."

"Yeah, I know, but so is William, and if he has gone after your father then I am so sorry," concluded the servant. Madelyn looked up at the castle that was looming above them and saw that the light in the guest room where William was sleeping was on. "Oh no," whispered Madelyn charging out of the stables and across the courtyard. Madelyn swung the entrance doors to the castle open, this time not caring if she awoke anyone and charged up to the room where William was staying. Madelyn reached the corridor where William was sleeping and saw a man with a blue cloak flung over him walk out of William's room. She stared in horror as she saw a red substance drip from under the man's cloak. As the man passed she scanned him with her eyes to find out where the red substance was coming from. She saw a knife clutched in the man's hand dripping with fresh blood. Her heart pounded, her breathing quickened. Had this man murdered William? If he had, then she had to stop him before he murdered Cameron as well. She stepped out of the shadows and ran over to the man in hope of tackling him from behind but he turned around and in one swift move of his fist, the princess lay unconscious.

The Peace Treaty

Madelyn woke up not remembering any of the events from the previous night. She sighed, it was five hours until the peace treaty was to be signed and the cities of Lemuria and Greenmont would become brothers in arms. Madelyn's servant came through the door and said, "Rise and shine your highness, today is a big day."

"Don't remind me," grumbled Madelyn.

"You don't seem too happy about it," remarked the servant turning around from opening the purple embroidered curtains, "I know you think your father doesn't love you but he does. He does all this to protect you otherwise he wouldn't ask William to sign the treaty. So just remember your father loves you and he always will."

"I suppose you're right," said Madelyn swinging out of her bed, her eyes trying to adjust to the light of her room. Madelyn looked over to her window and saw a strong firm hand clutched to the windowsill on the outside. "Who's that?" she said rushing over to the window and flinging it open. Madelyn jumped back just in time as a sharp point of a sword was thrust through the window opening. Then a man dressed fully in black leapt through the window with a sword clutched firmly in his hand. The terrified servant backed up against the wall. The intruder swung the sword again but Madelyn was able to evade the attack. Madelyn's servant, recovering from his frightened state, charged at the man and hit him on the nose shouting, "That was for my mistress." The man just stared angrily at the servant before swiftly slicing his sword across the servant's face. Madelyn watched in horror as her servant's blood sprayed across the floor. She ran towards her bed and pulled a long sharp sword decorated with shiny red rubies on the hilt, out from under it. The sword wore Lemuria's royal seal which was a sword surrounded by a ring of fire. Madelyn had never used a sword before. She had only stolen it from the armoury because she might get attacked and like so many other things she was right.

Although frightened, she ran over to the man and slashed her sword at him. However, the man countered her blow before forcing her back against the wall. Clearly a highly skilled swordsman, he seemed to have been doing this all his life. As the encounter pursued, Madelyn soon became weak and the man was able to disarm her. Her sword slid across the stone floor to the other side of the room. The man's attention turned to the servant bleeding heavily from his wound as he crawled across the cold, hard floor. Realising what was about to happen Madelyn screamed, "NO!" as she watched the man bring his sword down into her servant's chest.

The man, hearing Cameron's footsteps, made his exit through the still open window. Cameron burst into the room and immediately ran over to his daughter who was shaking uncontrollably. "Oh, my daughter," said Cameron taking his beloved in his arms and trying to steady her shaking, "Are you alright?"

"Am I alright?" exclaimed Madelyn breaking away from her father's embrace. "What about him?" She waved her hand towards the floor where her servant lay groaning earnestly in pain. Cameron glanced at the servant briefly before saying, "He's a servant, his life expendable."

"How can you say that?" said Madelyn, "He saved my life."

"I am well aware of that," Cameron said putting his hand on his daughter's shoulder, "The best I can do is give him a dignified send off."

"A dignified send-off," said Madelyn once again breaking away from her father's grasp, "No, that's not good enough he needs proper treatment – a cure."

"A cure that I cannot provide," said Cameron staring at Madelyn, with eyes that gave away nothing, "Now that you are alright I must meet with my people in the throne room."

"What! You can't possibly continue with the peace treaty?" said Madelyn. Not waiting for a reply she continued, "How can you think about that at a time like this! Or have you already forgotten that a man tried to kill me?"

"No, I am well aware of what has happened and the man will be found and executed," said Cameron with an angry edge to his voice, "But until then we cannot allow hesitation because our enemies will take it as weakness and that means war. So I have to continue the signing of the peace treaty no matter what." Madelyn, with saddened eyes, watched her father leave the room.

William was waiting when Cameron strode into the throne room. Cameron had never signed a peace treaty because he always thought people could never be forgiven but for his daughter's sake he had to make sure it went well. When Cameron reached the other side of the room, where there was a temporary table set up, he shook hands with William. "Let's get this over with," said Cameron gesturing to the peace treaty. Sir William turned around looking at it for a moment considering if he should sign it or not, but in the end he did.

Violet and Madelyn

After the signing of the peace treaty Madelyn was to be found upon the green and peaceful castle grounds staring out at the skyline and wondering about her servant's wellbeing. The sword had gone in quite deep and Madelyn still couldn't believe that her servant had taken that blow for her. She sat down on the grass, which was a little bit wet from the morning dew, but she didn't care. She just needed time to think about the last day's events. "Care if I join you?" said a friendly voice behind her - it was her friend Violet.

"No, take a seat," said Madelyn gesturing to a fairly dry patch of grass and Violet sat down. "You seem to have something on your mind again," noticed Violet.

"Well in case you hadn't realised, earlier today a man broke into my room and tried to kill me," said Madelyn, a little sharper than she meant to. Violet looked pained.

"Sorry," said Madelyn, "I just have a lot on my mind."

"I know, but I can help you," sympathised Violet.

"No I prefer to figure things out on my own," said Madelyn.

"But, I can help you Madelyn," said Violet.

"I don't need your help," snapped Madelyn. Violet could not hide the pained expression but Madelyn didn't seem to notice or didn't care. "Madelyn, I know how you feel," empathised Violet.

"No you don't. You can't even begin to understand," shouted Madelyn getting up and leaving.

Madelyn went and sat down on a rock which protruded from the ground on the shore of the moat, which flowed around the circumference of the city. Madelyn didn't mean to have hurt

Violet's feelings but she just didn't want to admit that she wa. angry. She was scared. I suppose with being a princess she wou get used to all these deaths and terrifying things that seemed to occur a lot in the castle these days, but she didn't want to. She knew dark days were coming and then everything would be different. Madelyn listened to the rushing sound of the water going over the rocks on the river bed and lay her head back on the grass and drifted off to sleep.

"There you are," said a voice that snapped her out of her deep sleep. She was having such a great dream as well. She dreamt that she was flying over the city of Lemuria and that everything looked so peaceful, that it almost looked real. She shook her head. 'It was just a dream,' she thought. The person who had woke her out of her sleep was Violet. She was wearing a different dress to the last time Madelyn had seen her. This one was purple with yellow flowers on it and there were no sleeves. The dress was frayed at the shoulders. "The King has been searching everywhere for you," continued Violet. 'Oh great,' Madelyn thought to herself, 'That's all I need.' Violet saw a worried look flash over Madelyn's face before she knelt beside her in encouragement and said, "It will be all right, your father probably just wants to talk to you about the celebrations that are coming."

"Boring," muttered Madelyn. Violet let out a little laughter before holding out her hand and saying, "Come on." Violet helped Madelyn up off the floor and they set off through the castle grounds and back to the castle. Madelyn felt relieved that Violet seemed to have forgotten about their little argument yesterday. She didn't want to have that to add to the stress she was already suffering. As they arrived at the castle Violet turned to Madelyn, "This is where I leave you, the King awaits you in his private quarters," she said.

"Thank you Violet," said Madelyn.

"What for?" asked Violet.

A smile flickered on Madelyn's face, "For everything," she replied.

Madelyn entered the King's quarters and her eyes immediately started to adjust to the darkness. There were no lights in the room apart from one candle that lay in the centre where there was a table. At the table sat Cameron and William and they were talking about something. "You see if anyone defies me then they are straight to the gallows," said William as if he hadn't seen Madelyn come in.

"Now that is exactly my point," said Cameron taking a sip of the dark red liquid that was in his goblet, which Madelyn assumed was wine, "There is too much bad in this world. It must be wiped out, no room for kindness." As Madelyn stared at William a dull throbbing started in her head like a painful memory that she was failing to remember. There was something about William that she had to tell the King, but what was it? "Madelyn," exclaimed William becoming aware of her presence in the room. "Sorry," she said feeling like she had intruded on something she shouldn't have, "My father said he wanted to see me."

"And I do," said Cameron pushing his chair and Madelyn flinched at the sound of it scraping across the floor, "Come with me." Cameron guided Madelyn towards the door before informing William, "We will be back in a minute."

"I understand my friend," said William holding up his goblet with a smile that seemed forced.

"So what do you need?" asked Madelyn.

"Well I think some celebrations are in order for our miraculous achievement, so I want you to tell all the men to get ready for a three-day jousting competition," said Cameron.

"Father I don't think that's wise," protested Madelyn.

"And why is that?" asked Cameron.

"It's just…" Madelyn shook her head, what was she going to say? "It's nothing," said Madelyn.

"Good," said Cameron, "Now go and tell the men that the competition will be starting tomorrow and they need to prepare."

"Will do father," said Madelyn and then Cameron walked back into his quarters.

As Madelyn made her way down the stairs to meet up with Violet her head felt heavy. She had meant to tell Cameron something; something she needed to remember but she couldn't. Madelyn looked up and instead of Violet standing there, it was William. He stood erect with his hand on his sword. He then let out a menacing laugh and Madelyn's legs gave way beneath her.

Hospital

Madelyn woke up on a smooth and comfortable surface. Laid across her was a white cloth that was stained with red marks; blood. But that wasn't the worst thing; the worst thing was that Madelyn saw that the blood was coming from her. 'Oh my goodness,' she thought, sitting up quickly and finding herself in the hospital. "Don't move," said a voice. The doctor ran over to her and assessed Madelyn's blood stained hand. "You should be ok for now," said the doctor wrapping Madelyn's hand in a clean white bandage, "I think you need to stay here for a few more days though."

"What happened?" asked Madelyn.

"No one knows exactly," said the doctor continuing to dress the wound on Madelyn's hand. "Your friend, Violet, says that you were walking down the stairs and then you started shaking uncontrollably. The next thing she knew was that you had stumbled and fallen down the stairs, unfortunately landing on something sharp which no doubt caused the wounds."

"Where is Violet?" asked Madelyn looking round the room hoping to find Violet standing in the shadows. "She went to get the king," said the doctor, "He should be on his way now," As if on cue the door opened and Violet entered the room, followed by Cameron. As soon as Cameron saw Madelyn laid on the bed he rushed over to her bed side. "Are you ok? Oh my goodness, are you ok?" said Cameron trembling.

"I'm fine father," said Madelyn.

"Violet told me what happened," said Cameron suddenly sounding angry, "How could you be so foolish."

"I'm sorry father, it was an accident," said Madelyn disappointedly, as her father seemed to care more about his reputation and not the state that his daughter was in, "I don't know what came over me."

"Well you need to be stronger as a person or you will never be worthy of the throne," said Cameron getting up and walking out. "I sometimes feel that I will never impress him," said Madelyn voicing her concerns. "He's just got a lot on his mind," said the doctor. Madelyn turned to look at the doctor. There he was again, in the doctor's place, William! Madelyn let out a high pitched shriek and shouted, "Get away from me."

"Madelyn," said William rushing over to her.

"Stay away from me," said Madelyn inching her way up the bed trying to get as far away from William as possible. It wasn't enough as William grabbed her roughly by the shoulders and started shaking her while shouting, "Madelyn." 'It's just a dream' thought Madelyn closing her eyes. When she opened them again her eyes came into contact with the doctor who looked worried. "What happened?" asked Madelyn trembling.

"It may be just a reaction to the accident," said the doctor.

"But it was very real," said Madelyn. She couldn't stop trembling. The night before the peace treaty was signed, it was all coming back to her. She had seen a man, the most terrifying man in all of creation with crimson blood dripping from his short, straight dagger that was fresh from a recent murder. Who had the man murdered that day? At the time she had thought that he had killed William, but now she knew that wasn't true because she had seen William talking to the king in his private quarters. What if William was the murderer? "Madelyn," said the nurse cutting through her train of thought, "You need rest."

"I'm fine," said Madelyn. Madelyn turned to look at Violet but she no longer wore those friendly and kind eyes that she had grown used to, instead Violet looked at her like she was a poor, pathetic creature from a mental asylum. "Can you give us some time alone," Violet said to the doctor.

"She needs rest," said the doctor.

"Please," begged Violet. The nurse didn't look too happy about it but in the end she stood up and said, "Okay, five minutes but no longer." With those words she strode to the far side of the office to check on her other patient, Madelyn's servant. "Madelyn," said Violet putting a gentle hand on Madelyn's shoulder, "What's up, you can tell me I'm your friend."

"You wouldn't believe me," said Madelyn.

"Try me," said Violet, a smile dancing across her face.

"I think William means to kill my father," said Madelyn.

"Do you have any evidence to support this?" whispered Violet.

"No," said Madelyn.

"Then don't worry about it," replied Violet. "Anyway, I came to say that I will be away for a few months because I'm helping one of my friends out in the kingdom."

"Don't go," whispered Madelyn, but Violet was already gone.

Celebrations

"In celebration of the signing of the peace treaty," said Cameron addressing the crowd, "we will be hosting a three-day jousting competition and the winner will be bestowed with the honour of escorting my daughter to the feast."

The crowd cheered loudly and it took Cameron about a minute to calm the excited outburst down. "So let the competition begin!" exclaimed Cameron and the crowd cheered again.

First to take up the challenge were Andrew and George. George was dressed in blue and he wore the crest of Greenmont, whereas Andrew, dressed in black, wore the crest of Lemuria, which was a diamond decorated skull. "You know the rules," said Cameron looking down at the two warriors. "First person to knock the other off their horse wins. 1-------2------3 begin!"

The warriors charged at each other and Cameron watched with anticipation as the warriors drew closer to each other. Andrew acted first by swiftly swinging his spear across George's head making him clutch his horse tightly for support. George reached the other side of the field and still hadn't fallen off his horse. Alternatively, Andrew unscathed, just looked at him with a confident face before they charged again. Andrew wore a nasty grin as he prepared to deliver his final blow but at the last second George swiftly leaned away from the attacking blow and brought his spear up striking Andrew in the face. Andrew flipped backwards off his horse and broke his leg, with a nasty crunch, as he landed on the soft sand. George stopped his horse short and jumped off it to the sounds of the knights of Greenmont cheering. Cameron gave out a long sigh as he really wanted a knight of Lemuria to win the tournament because he didn't want any of those pathetic men dressed in blue pretending to be knights taking his daughter to the feast.

Five more rounds followed and two of them were won by knights of Lemuria and the other three were won by knights of Greenmont. Cameron told everyone that the competition would continue that afternoon and then he and Madelyn made their way into the castle. "Our men need more training. I can't believe they could lose like that," said Cameron.

"Let me train them," said Madelyn.

"No," said Cameron, "Fighting is a man's job so I must see to it myself."

"I could help," protested Madelyn.

"I said no," said Cameron turning around to face her. "Why don't you go to your room, I need to have a word with William." Madelyn went to her room and flung her pillow in anger. How could her father be like this, she thought he cared. The only two people who truly understood were Violet and her servant. Violet was out of town and her servant was in the hospital, so she could talk to neither of them. "Oh my," she whispered to herself as she felt the tears flow down her cheeks, "I hate him so much. He still treats me like a child."

She looked on the floor and saw a sword; the exact sword she had used to fend off the intruder from the previous week and the point was smothered in blood. Madelyn heard a scream and then a ripping noise followed by the thud of something hitting the floor. Madelyn shook her head but she couldn't shake off the memory of the man looking at her, his hands tainted with her servant's blood, that unbearable laugh shaking the walls of her room. She snapped out of the memory and stared at the sword with a solemn expression. She kicked the sword under her bed so she didn't have to look at it and keep the constant reminder and the stabbing pain of that dreadful memory. She walked over to the window and opened it. Maybe the warmth of the sun would take her mind off things. She leaned out of the window dangerously far and looked out across the city of Lemuria and saw the crowd of people in the market chattering to their friends and having a good time.

Later that day, Madelyn returned to the hospital. She saw the doctor and walked over to him. "How is he?" she asked. "You can ask him yourself," said the doctor leading his over to the back of the room where her servant lay looking paler than the last time she had seen him. "How are you?" she asked.

"I`ve been better," said the servant forcing a smile. There was a flicker of a smile on Madelyn's face too but then she asked, "Why did you risk your life for me?"

"Because I believe in the Queen you are going to become but you're going to be no good to the city of Lemuria dead," said the servant.

"You didn't have to risk your life though," said Madelyn.

"Your life is worth a thousand of mine. I'm just a simple servant but you're the next heir to the throne of Lemuria and for that I don't mind the ice cold feel of death's embrace," said the servant.

"Look," said Madelyn, "We are going to find you a cure no matter what."

"It's over for me," said the servant looking up at her. "Don't risk your life for mine." The servant became unconscious and Madelyn got up wiping the tears from her cheeks. "Give him something to dull the pain," she said to the doctor, "I shall return."

Hunt for a Cure

Madelyn walked down the street and into a little corner shop named **Wilfred's Pills and Potions.** "Do you have anything for a sword wound to the stomach?" she asked before Wilfred had time to greet her. "I will see what I can find," he said standing up and coming over to one of the shelves which was filled with a plethora of potions and medicines. "I can't find anything that could be of any use," said Wilfred after scanning the shelves for a little while.

"There must be something we can use, anything, I don't care if I have to travel a thousand miles to get the cure I need. Just tell me where to find it."

"Well, there is one place you could look," said Wilfred instantly regretting it.

"Where is that?" asked Madelyn failing to contain the excitement in her voice.

"No it doesn't matter, it's too dangerous," replied Wilfred shaking his head.

"Just tell me please Wilfred," she demanded. Wilfred gave out a long sigh as he reached behind his desk and pulled out a big dusty book labelled **The Far Reaches**. Madelyn came over and looked at the book with interest while Wilfred scanned the pages trying to find what he was looking for. "Here," he said to Madelyn and she came over to see what he was pointing at, it was a picture of a small little town in a big plain. "In the Far Reaches of this land there is a plant called 'The Black Leaf' which has a completely black flower so it shouldn't be hard to find. It is the only thing that can heal close to death situations like a sword wound. If you bring me the flower I will be able to make the potion to heal your servant."

"How did you know it was for my servant?" said Madelyn looking up in puzzlement. "You're always disobeying your father's instructions so I just guessed that you would end up helping your servant." Madelyn looked at the floor, "Don't worry I won't tell him anything. I will stall for as long as I can, so get going."

"Thanks," said Madelyn rushing over to the door and pulling it open. She walked rapidly down towards the City gates. Then she saw the guards at the gates and she thought to herself, 'They will see me, I need a disguise.' She quickly went into the robe shop which was close by and bought a long, blue cloak with a hood. Something so plain that the guards wouldn't know it was her. "Hello," said one of the guards with a friendly wave. Madelyn tried her best to disguise her voice as that of a poor villager but it just came out like a little high-pitched squeak. The guards just watched her as she left the city shrugging their shoulders before returning to their post.

Madelyn made sure it was safe before pulling down her hood and clambering on to a horse. "Wait princess," said a voice behind her. She turned around and saw the guard who had greeted her earlier and so she turned back around and said, "Go," to the horse and the horse galloped off into the kingdom of Hells Rift.

"Sir," said the guard bursting into the throne room startling the king and the man with whom he was talking - the Captain of the Guard, John Nessle. "Haven't you learned to knock boy," shouted John looking at the guard with a look of disgruntled disgust.

"But this is important," said the guard, "It's about Madelyn."

The king signalled John to stay silent and when he didn't reply the king turned to the guard and said, "What about Madelyn?"

"She has run away," replied the guard.

"What do you mean by 'she has run away'?" asked the king.

"I mean she has got herself on a horse and galloped off into the kingdom," said the guard. The king's eyes widened but then he said to John. "She can't have gone far. Send a search party compiled of your best men to see if you can find her."

"Whatever you say your majesty," said John, running out of the throne room and down into the barracks. The king turned towards the guards and then said, "I need you to go with him and make sure he brings Madelyn back in one piece."

"Yes sir," said the guard following John out of the throne room.

Madelyn didn't look back, she just galloped on and on trying to get as far away from the city as possible before her father sent out a search party. The horse started to slow down to a trot so Madelyn guided it under the cover of some trees that lay next to a river. She then took one look back to see how far she had come and saw the tallest tower of Lemuria rising up in the distance.

The Search Party

"You know the drill," said John pacing in front of the three men that he had picked, "Find the princess and bring her back alive. Do I make myself clear?"

"Yes sir," chorused the guards.

"Good," said John walking over to a horse, "then let's go." John and his guards mounted their horses and set off into the kingdom in synchronicity. "She couldn't have gotten far," said John after a little while. "There," said a guard pointing to a billow of smoke rising from the trees about three mile ahead of them. "Head for those trees," ordered John and his men obeyed, galloping for the trees with the wind blowing in their faces. Madelyn saw them coming, she quickly got up and stamped the fire out. She picked up the sword, she had brought from her room, off the dirty and grimy floor of the forest. She sped over to where the horse was tethered to the tree and sliced the rope. "Go," she whispered to the horse but it wouldn't budge. "You have to run, I will meet you at the next town," said Madelyn and the horse listened this time.

Madelyn found a concealed spot and lay there as the men came into the clearing. "She must have been here," said John kneeling down to inspect the fire. "That could be anyone's fire," said one of the guards. John inspected the coal and then said, "It's just been put out, it's definitely hers," John rose to his feet. "We know you're out there princess. We are here to bring you home."

Madelyn held her breath so that she would not be found and she retracted further into the trees when she heard a growling noise behind and something sharp pressing into her spine. It was a jaguar. Madelyn didn't care if she was caught. She had to have help so she didn't try to hold back the scream. "That's her," said John rushing over to the trees but before he reached them the jaguar jumped onto him. "Aaaaggggggghhhhhh" he screamed as the weight of the jaguar pushed him onto the floor. "I'm on my way sir," said one of the guards coming over and swiping his sword at the jaguar. But the jaguar just swiped his claws up and knocked the guard back into a tree. The force killed him instantly. Madelyn made herself visible to the jaguar and she made it follow her trampling two other guards in the process. Now it was just her and John.

The jaguar started to make its way forward letting out long, low, rumbling growls. "Get away from the princess!" shouted John, swiping his sword at the jaguar but it dodged and turned around. In long swift swipe of its claws John was on the floor covered in blood. "Noooooooo!" screamed Madelyn running forward and jumping onto the jaguar's back. Before it had realized where she was she sliced her sword down into its back and made sure it stayed there until she felt the jaguar go stiff and fall to the floor. Madelyn let go of the hilt of the sword as she tumbled off the jaguar's back with a thump. "Princess," a voice croaked in front of her. Madelyn looked up and saw John with blood trickling from his lip and a good sized cut across his abdomen was leaking blood. "John," the princess croaked back.

"I know why you came. You want to help him. Your servant because he saved you. You are so unlike your father which is really wonderful but I don't think you will be able to make it alone."

"I'm fine really," whispered Madelyn.

"No you aren't," said John his voice faltering, "About one mile south of here there is a town. Ask for Richard and he will be able to help you find what you are looking for."

"I will consider it," said Madelyn, a slight smile appearing on her lips.

"That's good, now I just want you to make me one last promise," said John.

"You make this sound like its goodbye," said Madelyn her smile faltering.

"Just promise me that you will become the queen that I know you can be. I am just sad that I won't be there to see you become that person. So promise me that you will do what your heart tells you and not your father. Then I can die in happiness," John's heartbeat ceased and he slumped to the ground, dead.

"I promise," whispered Madelyn. She got up and started to make her way in the direction of the city. When she made her way out of the cover of the trees the town was in plain sight. When she arrived in the town she heard a woman shouting, "Stop it you horrible man." Madelyn rushed towards the shouting and from behind a wooden building she spotted a man standing there with his sword out in front of him, swinging it around like he was insane. The man looked a little older than Madelyn, had black hair, tanned skin and piercing dark eyes. He didn't look like he was from anywhere around the area, for his torn clothes weren't of any familiar tailor and his arms looked ravaged. There wasn't anything near here that could do that to such a tall and muscular young man. The man was laughing at the woman's fear. Madelyn had to stop it before something bad happened. "HEY!!!" she shouted stepping into the alleyway. The man turned and saw Madelyn which made him laugh even more. "And who may you be?" asked the man. "I am a woman who wants what is right, so let her go," said Madelyn sounding more confident then she felt inside. The man looked surprised at Madelyn's nonchalance but then he just simply said, "No." Madelyn got angry and unsheathed her sword which was still stained with jaguar blood and growled, "Then I'll fight you."

"If you say so," said the man with a little giggle, also unsheathing his sword. He swung first knocking Madelyn back. He ran towards her and swung again but she ducked and stepped to the right bumping into a house. The man brought the sword down and Madelyn managed to move her head to the side just in time and the man's sword stuck into the wood. Madelyn had to do something, if she didn't she would die. She'd never used a sword in battle but she had to try if it meant it would save innocent people. Madelyn kicked him in the chest and he lost his grip on the sword as he tumbled to the ground. He was at her mercy - she could finish it. Madelyn lifted her sword up and while doing that she looked into the man's eyes. She couldn't do it. She could not intentionally harm a man or woman no matter what they had done. "Stop," screamed Madelyn dropping her sword to the floor before falling to her knees, "Please stop." The man picked Madelyn up and slammed her into the wall and Madelyn heard the sound of the wood splintering behind her. "Why did you call off the fight, too scared?" sneered the man. "I won't hurt you," said Madelyn.

The man let go of her and said, "You have been brought up well," said the man, "What's your name?" Madelyn remembered what her father had told her when she was little, that names carry power. They can be the destruction of cities or the birth of civilisations. "My name's Natalie," lied Madelyn.

"That's a good name," said the man, all the violence that had clouded his eyes was nowhere to be seen, "Mine's Richard." This was Richard? Madelyn couldn't believe it. This was the person that John had promised would be able to help her find the cure. He couldn't be. "So you're Richard," was all Madelyn could bring herself to say.

"Yeah, have you heard of me?" asked Richard.

"We need to talk," said Madelyn gesturing to an alley between two buildings. They both went into the darkness of the alley. "A friend of mine said that you would be able to help me find what I am looking for," said Madelyn.

"Who is he?" asked Richard.

"His name was John. He said that you two were close," said Madelyn.

"We were," said Richard looking at the ground, "Where is he now?"

"He's dead," breathed Madelyn, the realization of it only just starting to sink in.

"I'm sorry," whispered Richard, "he was a good man."

"Yeah I know, but down to the point - he said you could help me," said Madelyn.

"Depends what you need help with," said Richard.

The Route

"I need a plant called Black Leaf and I know it's in the far reaches of the land," said Madelyn. "Do you know what part of the far reaches it is in?" asked Richard.

"Not exactly," replied Madelyn.

"Then how do you expect to find it then?" asked Richard.

"John said you would be able to help," said Madelyn.

"I have an idea," said Richard. "There could be some near the town of Littleleaf but you won't make it alone. I will come with you."

"I can do this on my own," said Madelyn.

"I am well aware of that but any friend of John is a friend of mine and I can't take the risk and let you go out there on your own."

"Okay," said Madelyn. "Meet me at the tavern entrance at sunrise and then we will get going."

"Ok I will be there," said Richard.

When Madelyn arrived she found Richard waiting for her. "What exactly do you need this plant for?" asked Richard.

"It's classified," said Madelyn, walking down the street. Richard realising that he wasn't going to get an answer, walked reluctantly after her. People kept staring at them as they passed with confused looks. "What was the princess doing with a mere peasant?" the people asked each other as they watched the weird duo walk down the street.

"So I think we should head towards the town of Littleleaf which is in the area of all the healing plants. I take it the black leaf should be there," said Richard as they walked down the street. "Then what are we waiting for?" said Madelyn quickening her pace.

"Not so fast," said Richard catching up to her. "We can't just go stumbling blindly into the Far Reaches. The books say they are inhabited by many dangerous creatures."

"But those are just stories," replied Madelyn.

"I think you and I both know that they aren't just stories, they are very, very true," stated Richard. Madelyn shrugged Richard's hand off her shoulder and said, "I don't care if they are true or not. Nothing is getting in the way of me and that plant. And if anything or anyone tries I will kill it."

Madelyn continued on her way but then took a right turn instead of heading for the outskirts of the city. "Where are you going?" asked Richard, who was confused by the sudden change in direction. "There is something I have got to do first," replied Madelyn. Madelyn made her way towards the town's stables and when she got to the door she turned around to Richard and said, "Just stay here I will be back in a moment."

"But what are you doing, going into the stables?" queried Richard.

"You will find out soon," said Madelyn, disappearing into the stables and reappearing about two minutes later holding the reins of two horses. One was her own and the other was the one she had found next to her horse. "You can't expect us to go on a long journey without some form of transport," said Madelyn seeing Richards's confused look.

"I suppose not," said Richard as Madelyn hopped onto her horse and then Richard came over and hopped onto the other. "Are you ready?" Madelyn asked Richard.

"As ready as I'll ever be," replied Richard.

Madelyn set off at a gallop as Richard followed her into the plains. The plains were more stunning than Madelyn had ever imagined. She had never left the castle before because her father forbade it under any circumstances but now she had finally done it, she had finally found the strength to disobey her father and run off into the picturesque setting of the plains. "Wow this is wonderful," said Madelyn as her scarlet hair flew in the wind. "I take it this is your first time away from the castle," said Richard smiling at Madelyn's enjoyment. "Yes," said Madelyn pushing her hair out of her face, "And it's wonderful." Madelyn and Richard rode into the plains unaware of the many dangers that awaited them.

The Dangerous Plains

Richard came over and threw a few more sticks on the already sizzling fire. "That's it for today. Let's get some rest and we will set off first thing in the morning," he said.

"Thanks," said Madelyn resting her head on the grassy floor of the plains. Exhausted, she was soon asleep.

In the depths of her dreams, Madelyn made her way into the courtyard and observing a pile of wood in its centre. "Get off me you creeps!" shouted a man to her right as he was pulled towards the pile of wood by two guards. Madelyn just stood and watched as the man was tied to a plank of wood that stuck out of the top of the pile. "You will pay for this," said the man as he watched a guard walk towards the pile of wood with a wooden torch that was already lit. "I will come back from the other world and haunt you." The guard threw his flaming torch into the pile and Madelyn watched with a scared gaze as the man just laughed as he was engulfed in flames.

Madelyn woke in cold sweat and immediately observed her surroundings. She was still in the plains and not too far away she saw Richard standing guard. Richard turned around and saw her awake and then his gaze set upon the scared look in her eyes. "Oh my goodness, Madelyn, are you okay?" he asked as he rushed over to her side.

"Yeah, I'm fine," lied Madelyn.

"Ok," said Richard, "well, seen as though you are awake we should get going." It only took five minutes to pack up camp and then they were on the road again. It was going to be a very long day. Madelyn's heart pounded as she heard the simultaneous knocking of her horse's hooves. After a little while Madelyn heard a howl in the distance. "What was that?" she asked slowing her horse down to a halt. "I don't know," said Richard turning pale with fright. A figure appeared in the trees. It was a large animal and it was making its way towards them at a slow pace. "It can't be," Madelyn whispered to herself.

"A werewolf," confirmed Richard. Madelyn stared in horror as the werewolf got increasingly closer. She felt the darkness close in on her as she stared at those luminous green eyes. Werewolves weren't real, they were just a myth, and a story to make children behave. But what Madelyn saw before her was very real. Madelyn's horse bucked, throwing Madelyn onto the grass in plain sight of the werewolf. Madelyn rolled to the side as the werewolf came barrelling past. She stood up and drew her sword while she stood and faced the werewolf. "Madelyn are you insane?" said Richard clambering down from his horse, "That's a werewolf."

"But it's still just an animal," replied Madelyn as the werewolf charged again. Madelyn got ready to swipe her sword but she was too late. The werewolf slashed its claws across her arm and she stumbled to the ground. Once she was on the floor the werewolf jumped onto her and opened its big gaping mouth. 'Oh no,' thought Madelyn because she knew what was going to come next. Richard jumped down off his horse and ran to Madelyn's rescue hitting the werewolf with the butt of his sword. It didn't seem to have done any real damage but at least it had got it off Madelyn.

Madelyn stood up and saw the werewolf ready to charge but this time Madelyn was ready for it. As it jumped up at her once more, she swung her sword slashing through its furry skin. The werewolf gave out a whining howl as it tumbled onto the grassy plain and Madelyn just watched the grass turned to a shade of crimson as the werewolf leaked blood. "That was a werewolf! A real werewolf," stuttered Richard. As he stared down at the corpse the werewolf amazingly turned back into the form of a dead and bloodied man.

Richard knelt down in sadness and closed the man's eyes with a gentle touch while whispering, "Rest in peace."

"That doesn't matter we need to get moving," said Madelyn. "There is no time for hesitation." Madelyn felt a sharp pain shoot through her shoulder and she clutched it trying not to show any sign of weakness to Richard, but it didn't work. "Are you alright?" asked Richard.

"I'm fine," snapped Madelyn.

"I wouldn't be so sure," said Richard, gently removing her hand from her shoulder. Madelyn looked for the first time at the damage that the ghastly beast had made and she immediately felt faint. Richard lunged forward and grabbed Madelyn as her legs buckled underneath her. "Don't die," said Richard, "Oh please don't die."

"I'm fine Richard," said Madelyn standing up but immediately stumbling back to the ground. Richard knelt next to her and said, "You need rest."

"But I need that flower," protested Madelyn in a weary tone.

"You will be no good on the quest like this," replied Richard.

"I suppose you're right," said Madelyn slumping to the ground as her vision faded into blackness.

Not Giving Up

Madelyn's head was spinning as she started to see trees swim into view. "Where am I?" she whispered to herself. Then she remembered: the werewolf, her shoulder, Richard leaning over her. Oh it was terrifying, so terrifying. "Glad to see you awake," said a voice to her left and she saw Richard step into her line of sight. "How long have I been out?" asked Madelyn. "Five days," replied Richard.

"What!" shouted Madelyn, throwing off the blanket that had been laid gently on her and standing up. "Why didn't you wake me?"

"I needed to wait for you to gain a full recovery," replied Richard.

"Well, then we need to get going now," said Madelyn picking her sword from the floor and walking off into the trees. Richard just stood there and said, "You're so determined to risk your life for this flower. I have never seen someone show such loyalty to one person."

"The person in question saved my life," said Madelyn turning to face Richard. "And he almost gave his life in the process and I won't let him die so therefore I need that flower."

"But do you actually know what to do with this flower once you've got it?" asked Richard.

"No, but I know someone who does," replied Madelyn.

They spent the whole day walking up huge hills and making their way along treacherous cliff edges stopping at regular intervals - but that was usually Madelyn waiting for Richard to catch up.

They stopped to have a sleep but then the next day they got straight back up and set off again. Late into the afternoon Madelyn was once again watching Richard as he struggled to climb up the hill. "I can't go on," croaked Richard, exhausted and gasping for breath, "We need to rest."

"We can't," said Madelyn turning around.

"Madelyn," said Richard "Take a break. We can't go on like this otherwise we will be too exhausted to fight if we get attacked."

Madelyn looked at the floor and whispered, "I don't want to lose him."

"I understand that," sympathised Richard staggering towards her, "but we need rest."

"Ok," said Madelyn leading him over to a shady spot underneath a solitary tree that was right next to them, "I will stand guard for now."

"Ok, thanks Madelyn," said Richard lying down on the ground and instantly falling asleep. Madelyn knelt down next to Richard and whispered, "I'm so sorry but I need that flower." Madelyn stood up and made her way towards the nearest town which was the town of Stoneville.

Madelyn walked through the bustling crowds of Stoneville. As she tried to make her way towards the town centre, a voice behind her whispered, "Madelyn?" Madelyn turned around and was shocked to see Violet standing there with a confused look on her face. "What are you doing here?" asked Violet.

"I could ask you the same thing," said Madelyn giving Violet a quick hug.

"I came to help a friend in need. She was having trouble with managing her crops so I agreed to help her," replied Violet.

"Well I'm so glad I bumped into you because I need help but I can't discuss it here," said Madelyn.

"You can come back to my friend's house and then we can discuss matters there," said Violet. "Thanks," said Madelyn, following Violet through the overcrowded streets until they came to stand outside a big house with ornate wood designs on the side.

"Come in," said Violet holding the door open for Madelyn. Inside the house looked like a paradise. There were two big couches laid in the middle of a fairly big living room and on one of the couches sat a woman with long brown hair. "I bumped into one of my friends in the town centre and I said she could come here for a bit," said Violet to the woman on the couch while gesturing at Madelyn. The woman got up and bowed to Madelyn and when she raised her head she was smiling. "It's Princess Madelyn isn't it? My name's Mary and I'm Violets friend. It is an honour to have you as a guest in my house," she said.

"The pleasure is mine," said Madelyn giving Mary a friendly handshake. Then Mary remembered that she had left a stew on the stove and left the room leaving Violet and Madelyn alone. "So what are you doing here? It's not like Cameron to let you go this far," said Violet.

"He didn't. I needed something he couldn't provide and he wouldn't risk men to come and get it," replied Madelyn.

"So you're still the same old Madelyn," said Violet with a flicker of a smile, "always disobeying her father's instructions. Anyway, what are you looking for?"

"A cure," said Madelyn simply.

"A cure for who?" asked Violet her eyes widening.

"My servant," said Madelyn, pretending to look at the different decorations in the house so Violet wouldn't see that she was crying. "I don't have time to explain but I need that cure which is somewhere in the Far Lands."

"The Far Lands, you can't be serious," exclaimed Violet.

"I am. He saved my life so I don't care if I'm putting my life at risk. I will not give up on him," said Madelyn.

"What is this cure?" asked Violet.

"It's called the Black Leaf," replied Madelyn.

"Then something really bad must have happened to your servant if you want that plant," said Violet. "You're right. Something dreadful has happened and I need to get that flower as soon as possible so I need to get going."

Madelyn started to make her way for the door when from behind her Violet said, "The plains are even more dangerous at night. You can't just go out there, stay here for the night and then you can set back off in the morning."

"Ok," said Madelyn turning around and sitting on one of the couches which lay in the middle of the room.

Just One Day

Madelyn woke to a frantic knocking downstairs and then Violet came running in to the guest room. "There's someone here to see you," said Violet.

"Oh really," replied Madelyn, "Who?"

"He won't say," replied Violet. "All he will say is that he needs to speak to you urgently." "Alright I'm coming," groaned Madelyn as she swung out of bed. She put on her robe which lay next to the bed and made her way down stairs to see who could possibly be asking for her. It was Richard and he didn't look very happy. "How could you leave me like that?" shouted Richard while Madelyn stepped outside and shut the door behind her so they could have a talk in private. "I needed to continue the quest," said Madelyn.

"Well, you didn't get very far," said Richard.

"Yes, I know, but I saw a friend and decided to stay with her for the night. I will be back in a minute," said Madelyn disappearing back inside Mary's house and she found Violet dusting a very dusty mantelpiece. "Hi Violet," said Madelyn. "I need to get going."

"Yeah, I know, I heard the whole thing," said Violet standing up and turning to face Madelyn. "You're not going."

"I think you will find that I am," snapped Madelyn.

"Please Madelyn," said Violet a tear rolling down her cheek. "Listen to reason, it's too dangerous out there. Go back to the castle."

"I've come too far. I have to go on and anyway I won't abandon my servant," said Madelyn, turning to leave but Violet just came over and stood in the doorway.

"I won't let you go," stated Violet.

"Get out of the way," said Madelyn, trying to sidestep Violet but found Violet in her way again. "Please don't do this Madelyn. Have you ever stopped to consider the amount of danger you're walking in to?" said Violet.

"I'm sorry Violet," said Madelyn putting her hand on Violet's shoulder before walking past her and out of the door. "Good luck," whispered Violet watching Madelyn leave.

"Let's get going again," said Madelyn to Richard straightening up her robe and walking down the street while Richard followed her. "Wait Madelyn," he said stopping.

"What is it now?" she said frustrated by the fact that they had stopped again.

"Why don't we stay here for a while, take our minds off things?" said Richard.

"I would love to, but I can't," said Madelyn.

"Can't or won't?" said Richard.

Madelyn turned around and said, "Ok, but just for one day."

The Tavern

Madelyn and Richard entered the dingy local tavern which was filled to the brim with drunkards. There were some couples sitting down to have a drink and also what seemed to Madelyn like bandits in the corner of the room. Madelyn felt so out of place. It was nothing like the castle which she had become accustomed to, that was quiet, and sometimes a little lonely but she liked it that way. Whereas this place was packed full of people and there was a hundred voices echoing around the room. "I can't do this," said Madelyn, "There's too many people."

"There is a first time for everything," said Richard, holding his hand out towards Madelyn. "You`ll get used to it." Madelyn took his hand and let him lead her through the crowd of people to a table at the back which seemed to be the only table left. Madelyn sat down at the table and stared down the cramped space of the tavern. "Why did you bring me here?" asked Madelyn. "I have a feeling that you have lied to me. What could be so bad about your real name that you can't tell me?" asked Richard. "Natalie is my real name," said Madelyn lying once again. "Then why do you wear the crest of Lemuria?" asked Richard. Madelyn knew there was no getting out of this one, over the last few days she had grown attached to him and felt like she could trust him. "It's Madelyn," she said.

"Cameron's daughter," said Richard leaning across the table. "You do realise that you are the daughter of one of the most hated men in the entire kingdom. Anyway, thanks for telling me the truth, now that we have that sorted we need to go over our plans for the journey," said Richard. "I take it there is another reason why you brought me here," said Madelyn. Richard didn't answer, instead he got up and said, "I'm going to get some drinks, do you want anything?" asked Richard. "No I'm fine," said Madelyn and Richard went off into the crowds of the tavern. Madelyn understood why

Richard liked to come to places like this, it had a vibrant feeling to it and it made Madelyn want to forget all her troubles. She found all the arguments with her father, her servants dying face, the quest to the Far Lands, slipping out of her memory and lifting a weight from her shoulders. She could live the rest of her life here, she didn't have to go back to the castle and everything would be so much simpler here. Richard came back with a tankard of mead in his hand and put it on the table gently. "So Madelyn, tell me why you want this flower so badly," asked Richard.

"It's nothing," said Madelyn dismissively.

"I think I have a right to know," said Richard leaning across the table.

"My servant," gasped Madelyn, hurt by the words that had just escaped her lips. "My servant was stabbed and people are saying he's going to die but I won't let that happen." "Then let's make sure it doesn't," said Richard.

Lemuria's Greatest Enemy

They kept traveling for five hours without stopping for anything. "It's so much harder without horses," said Richard stumbling to the ground.

"I can't do anything about that," said Madelyn helping Richard back onto his feet, "We need to keep moving." Madelyn heard the sound of hooves behind her and turned around with amazement as their horses galloped towards them but they weren't alone. Two men were riding on the horses, armed with swords. As the horses closed the distance between them and Madelyn the two men jumped off and unsheathed their swords. "Oh no," said Richard pulling a knife out of his pocket and trying to fend one of the men off while Madelyn went for the other. The confrontation didn't last long and didn't end well, at least not for Madelyn and Richard. Madelyn swung her sword at the man but he countered it and disarmed her. The man struck Madelyn on the head with the hilt of his sword knocking her to the ground. She immediately tried to get back up but found the sharp point of the man's sword at her throat. Paralysed with fear, out of the corner of her eye, she saw Richard being beaten to the ground. "Well, well, well," said the man who had her at sword point, "If it isn't Princess Madelyn. You're a long way from home." With those words he struck Madelyn and she fell to the ground and lay there motionless.

Madelyn woke up on a grimy, cold stone floor. She saw Richard laid next to her with a severe head injury. "Richard!" exclaimed Madelyn, crawling over to him and checking his pulse. Madelyn heard a bolt being slid back behind her and then faint footsteps making their way towards her. "Well, so my men were right. We actually have captured Princess Madelyn! Oh, Cameron will pay handsomely for this," said a deep booming voice behind her. Madelyn felt a rough hand grab hold of her shoulder and force her to the floor. She tried not to cry as she felt her hands sting as they slammed against the floor. She turned around to have a look at the man and started crawling back towards the wall. The man had a big muscular figure and no hair and he wore the clothes of a servant. "Who are you?" cried Madelyn.

"Oh, but I am your father's greatest enemy. I am Galidion," exclaimed the man.

"You," gasped Madelyn. She remembered the name from a story that her father had told her when she was young and struggling to get to sleep because of the many nightmares that haunted her. The story went that Galidion had stolen many men and made the King furious causing a war. The war had gone on for a year with great losses on both sides including the men that had initially been stolen. Her father had felt nothing but rage upon the death of his men and had tried to confront Galidion in single combat. Cameron and Galidion had fought ferociously, neither surrendering to the other. Dead soldiers littered the barren wasteland of Hell's Rift as the battle raged on. Weary and battle worn Cameron succumbed to the power of Galidion, falling onto the ground of the bloodied wasteland of the battlefield. Galidion could not bring himself to deliver the final blow and spared him that day, a decision that no one could explain.

Madelyn snapped out of the memory and realised Galidion was saying something. "Yes it's me, your father took something from me so I have now taken something from him," said Galidion caressing Madelyn's cheek. "So what do you think your father will say when he realises I have taken his precious little girl?" Madelyn just stared at Galidion with a look of anger but inside she was petrified. Her father didn't know she was here, there was no help on its way, this time she really had done it. She had gone and got herself captured and possibly killed. Maybe she should have listened to her father. "What do you want from me?" asked Madelyn.

Galidion let out a small chuckle before saying, "Oh, it is not about what I want, it is about what I need."

"And what do you need?" asked Madelyn.

"Isn't it obvious, the thing I have desired all my life, the throne of Lemuria and with you in my clutches I am one step closer," said Galidion. Galidion left the cell while roaring with laughter and Madelyn just sank to the floor in despair.

Galidion was back that afternoon and he seemed to be happy with something. "Now I have finally done it! My greatest plan yet. I can already see that beautiful crown on my head and then Lemuria will be mine," said Galidion.

"W-w-what's going on?" stuttered Madelyn.

"Well, the king is under the impression that his lovely daughter is dead, with one messenger I have managed to drive the city of Lemuria into chaos and now that it's at its most vulnerable, this is the time for me to strike."

"You're insane," said Madelyn.

"Is Cameron any better?" asked Galidion. "I know what you think of him, I know you don't respect his decisions and that's why I am giving you a choice. Join me and help me build a better tomorrow."

Galidion held out his hand to Madelyn and for a second she felt compelled to accept his offer. There was some truth in what Galidion had said and she didn't respect some of her father's decisions. Maybe he did make radical and extreme decisions but he wasn't as crazy as this. "Get away from me," shouted Madelyn, slapping Galidion's away. Galidion watched Madelyn walk toward the other side of the room and then said, "Suit yourself."

Galidion walked out of the room and Madelyn, feeling scared and uncertain about what Galidion would do to get the throne, watched him leave. The whole of Lemuria was in trouble and there was nothing she could do about it. She looked at Richard who still lay on the floor and whispered, "Come on Richard, you'll know what to do, come on wake up." There was still no movement in Richard's lifeless body.

Funeral Arrangements

Cameron looked at the vacant room of his late daughter, Madelyn, and his thoughts were a world away. His Madelyn, his precious Madelyn was dead.

When the messenger had arrived in Lemuria and given the news that Madelyn had been killed by one of his most hated enemy's, Galidion, his heart had sunk. Camron walked over to Madelyn's dressing table and picked up a small hand mirror that lay there. It was the present he had given to her when she was six years old. Back then it was all shiny and sparkly, now it just looked dusty and old. Cameron put it back on the dressing table carefully and tried to put it in the exact place that it had been when he picked it up. Cameron wanted his daughter's room to stay exactly how it was when she had left it and it was going to stay that way for a very long time. Then Cameron turned to look at the bed and took in all the pieces of purple embroidery which lined the covers with sadness. The bed hadn't been slept in for about a week and it was never going to be slept in again, at least not by Madelyn.

"Sir," said a voice behind Cameron as a hand rested on his shoulder. "It's time." Cameron didn't say anything as he followed the man down to the courtyard at the front of the castle. Cameron observed the people of his city holding candles in commiseration to Madelyn, before his eyes fell on the jet black coffin which was going to be used for the ceremony. Feeling lost and empty his eyes started to well up with tears. "Start the proceedings," Cameron muttered reluctantly. Four guards of Lemuria made their way over to the coffin and with their combined strength they lifted it up above their heads and started to carry it down to the lake. The king joined the back of the crowd of hundreds of citizens and he followed the coffin with a sombre expression. They walked through the lifeless streets of Lemuria and more citizens started to join and more candles were lit in memory of Madelyn.

When they reached the lake Cameron saw that there was a boat already set out for the ceremony and he couldn't stop the flood of tears as he watched the coffin being loaded on to the boat. One guard came over with a bow and arrow and kicked the boat and it started to float of into the lake. The guard waited and watched until the boat was around the centre of the lake before striking his arrow to fire at the boat. Cameron watched as the boat was engulfed in flames from the arrow which had landed right on top of the coffin and set it alight.

"They want you to make a speech sir," said the man who had led Cameron down to the courtyard. Cameron stepped into view of all the citizens and said, "We are gathered here today to bid farewell to my daughter Princess Madelyn. It was only a few hours ago that we received a message saying that she had been murdered by our greatest enemy, Galidion. Many times I have wondered why Galidion chose to spare me on the plain that night but one thing is certain to me now. He will regret it! I will not rest until he has paid for everything he has done to my daughter. Galidion has committed high treason and for this crime he gives me no choice but to declare war!" The people of Lemuria cheered and that was the last time such joviality was heard for years to come.

Behind Bars

"Come on, come on," said Madelyn, putting her hands through the iron bars of the cell door and fumbling around for any sort of latch. If Madelyn was right, she and Richard had been in that stinking, rotting cell for about a week with no chance of escape. She kept thinking that Galidion would kill them but he didn't. There must be a bigger picture to Galidion's plan for power, but Madelyn couldn't find it. She heard guards making their way down the corridor towards the cell, so Madelyn stopped looking for a way to open the door and sat back down on the floor so they wouldn't think she was trying to escape. Two guards opened the cell door and threw a piece of bread in front of Madelyn. "Breakfast," announced one of the guards.

"I'm not eating that," said Madelyn looking down at the piece of bread in disgust.

"Well then, you'll starve," said the guard with a little laughter in his voice before exiting the room. As soon as they had left and went down the corridor Madelyn got up and started looking for a way to open the door again. "Nothing's indestructible," Madelyn whispered to herself trying to boost her self-esteem. No matter how much Madelyn kept telling herself that there was a way out she couldn't find it and her morale tumbled again. "What are you doing little girl?" said a booming voice. Madelyn looked up and saw Galidion standing there with a disapproving look on his face. Madelyn didn't answer and for her silence she paid dearly with a blow to the face. "No one escapes!" shouted Galidion.

"Are you sure about that" said Madelyn trying to sound brave and for that she suffered another blow from Galidion's fist. "Less of your cheek girl," said Galidion picking Madelyn up and throwing her into the wall. "You can do what you want to me but don't hurt my father," begged Madelyn. "Your father is already broken," sneered

Galidion. 'Oh no' Madelyn though to herself, 'What has he done to him?' "Now Lemuria will be mine," said Galidion.

Madelyn quickly got up onto her feet and aimed a punch at Galidion. He blocked it and then knocked her back down to the ground with one swift blow from his fist. "Your father will be dead soon and then we will see what you think about joining us," said Galidion, looking at Madelyn with a menacing face.

"I will never join you," growled Madelyn.

"We'll see about that," snorted Galidion before exiting the cell.

The next day Galidion returned with his hands behind his back striding into the room with undeniable pleasure. "Get up," he said to Madelyn, who was sat on the floor staring at him with a scared look in her eyes, as she realised Galidion's hostile intent. He removed his hands from behind his back and Madelyn saw that in his left hand he held a whip. He swung it down at Madelyn and she felt it hit her back knocking her to the ground. "What about now?" he said staring down at the dishevelled form of Madelyn.

"What are you?" asked Madelyn. Galidion flashed his whip down again now screaming in rage. "You don't get to ask questions! All you have to do is obey. Is that too much to ask?" roared Galidion.

"Yes," said Madelyn angering Galidion.

"Then maybe you need to be taught a lesson," said Galidion bringing his foot down with a thud.

Galidion

Everyday Galidion visited three times, once in the morning, once in the afternoon and once in the evening and everyday Madelyn grew weaker. On this particular day she was struggling to sit up because she was in that much pain, when Galidion appeared again. "On your feet princess," snarled Galidion, kicking Madelyn in the ribs. Before Madelyn could do anything, Galidion grabbed her and forced her against the wall. "Today is a very special day for me and I won't let you ruin it," said Galidion. Madelyn didn't say anything so Galidion gestured to two guards who were behind him and they came over and grabbed a shoulder each and lifted her onto her feet. "Take her to the pit," said Galidion before walking out of the cell. The two guards started to force Madelyn to the door when something lashed at one of the guards and he stumbled to the ground. Before the other guard realised what was happening a fist hit him causing him to fall to the floor in pain. Madelyn looked to see where the fist had come from and saw Richard standing there. He still had a pretty bad head injury but he seemed to be okay, which was more than could be said for Madelyn. "Come on we're getting out of here," said Richard walking over to her

"I can't," said Madelyn clearly in pain.

"You can," said Richard escorting Madelyn to the door which was now wide open. Richard scanned the corridor and there was no sign of any guards so he turned left and started to make his way down the corridor. They came to the end of the corridor and there was a corridor leading off to the right and another one leading off to the left. Richard took the left one. "You act as though you've got previous knowledge of this place," said Madelyn.

"No, I have never been here before in my life," replied Richard.

"Then how do you seem to know where we are going?" asked Madelyn.

"I am just guessing," said Richard. They approached the end of the second corridor which had only one corridor leading off it to the right. Richard peeked around the corner and quickly pulled his head back and then he put a hand on Madelyn's mouth before she could ask what was going on. A guard walked around the corner and Richard and Madelyn made their way into the shadows at the edge of the corridor hoping they would conceal them. The guard walked past and as soon as he could Richard broke his cover and hit him on the back of the head. Before the man hit the ground Richard unsheathed his sword and then pushed the man down. "Here you go," said Richard throwing Madelyn the sword. Madelyn caught it and said, "Thanks." The sword was plain and simple with a scratch on it near the point. It wasn't anything like Madelyn's sword but it was going to have to do.

The next guard they came to Madelyn quickly disarmed and gave the sword to Richard. Now that they were both armed they didn't have to be as careful as they made their way down the long corridors. They had almost reached the entrance when as they turned into the corridor they heard a voice behind them shout, "Catch the prisoners, don't let them escape!" Madelyn managed to turn around just in time to counter a blow from a man's sword as it came swinging down. Madelyn dodged the next one and disarmed the man as he tried to deliver the third blow. Before the guard could do anything Madelyn brought her sword down and stabbed the man through the chest. There was still about twenty men remaining and Madelyn knew she couldn't fight them all even with the help of Richard. "RUN!" shouted Madelyn, taking Richard's hand and leading him out of the door not looking behind because of fear of being caught.

Galidion came to the door as Richard and Madelyn disappeared over a hill in front of the building. "Change off plan," said Galidion turning to face his men. "You all go and march towards the city of Lemuria and I will catch up to you all. You can attack and destroy Lemuria all you want but with one exception. Leave Cameron for me. I want to deal with him myself but I have got his daughter to deal with first."

"You have to go back to Lemuria," said Richard.

"I still haven't go the flower and I need it to save my servant," replied Madelyn.

"Things have changed Madelyn, you heard what that madman said he's going after the throne of Lemuria and your father is pretty much defenceless you have to go back and help him," said Richard.

"My father is a strong man," said Madelyn, "he can hold out long enough for me to get back."

"What?" asked Richard.

"I need to do this alone," said Madelyn facing Richard. "It has been a great honour to have you on this journey and we will still meet again. You're right Lemuria does need help and you will be a greater help than me. Try and help him hold out until I get back."

"Madelyn, you can't," protested Richard.

"I'm sorry," said Madelyn kissing Richard gently on the lips, "Now go." Madelyn watched Richard set off back towards Lemuria before continuing on her journey.

In about a day Madelyn started to see a mountain range in the distance. "Maybe I could take cover in there," Madelyn whispered to herself, "There's bound to be a cave or something." She started to make her way across the plain towards the mountain with some difficulty. The sun was incredibly hot and the heat was starting to take effect on her but she didn't give up. She couldn't give up. Madelyn managed to make her way to the base of the nearest mountain and started to scan for a path. She found one that lead between two mountains.

Madelyn walked on down the mountain path when behind her she heard a voice get increasingly closer. "Madelyn come out. It will make it a whole lot easier for both of us," it said. 'Galidion' Madelyn thought to herself, rapidly scanning the surroundings for a place to hide. She found a cave entrance to her right. She rushed into it and went right to the back of the cave so that Galidion wouldn't see her in the darkness. Madelyn watched Galidion walk passed and gave a sigh of relief but then... "Did you really think you could escape me that easily?" said Galidion, stepping into the cave with his sword drawn. Madelyn drew her sword and quickly dodged as Galidion's sword crashed into the wall. Madelyn watched as a stone from the wall came down and crashed right through the floor leaving a gaping hole. 'The floors unstable' Madelyn thought to herself, dodging Galidion's sword once again. "You are just like you father," said Galidion, swiping at Madelyn again, but she jumped back. Madelyn felt the floor crumble and give way beneath her and she started to slowly fall through space. Madelyn quickly lashed out with her hand and managed to grab hold of the edge and she started to hold on for dear life. "There's nowhere to run Madelyn," said Galidion standing over her. "There is no helping Cameron. He must die, but I have no reason to kill you. Cameron has been influencing you for years but I can change that." Galidion knelt down and held out his hand for Madelyn to grab so he could help her up. Madelyn considered her options. It was either let Galidion help her up or let go and fall into the abyss. The hole might not even be that deep but she had no way of knowing without letting go and she didn't want to do that – however, she also didn't want to surrender to Galidion. "I'm sorry

Galidion but I can't take your offer," said Madelyn letting go of her handhold and plunging into darkness.

The Abyss

Madelyn kept on falling unable to hear anything but the wind blowing in her ears. There was a little bit of light but that wasn't going to last long. Madelyn watched the small circle of light, which was the hole in the cave floor, get smaller by the second. She kept scanning for any handholds but none were to be found. What was the point anyway? There was no way she was getting back up. Madelyn just closed her eyes and waited for the impact which was bound to happen anytime soon. But it didn't come. She just kept falling and falling with no sign of ground beneath her. Madelyn heard a splash and felt her back crack then her breath started to dissipate. 'Oh my, I'm dead' Madelyn thought to herself. 'But why does it hurt so much?' Madelyn opened her eyes and saw the misty scene of water clouding her vision. That was why she was struggling to breathe she was under water. She struggled from the water bed and burst through to the surface. Madelyn managed to crawl towards the ground at the side of the pool that she now lay in. She crawled out but then immediately stumbled to the ground coughing up water onto the floor. "Where am I?" Madelyn said rhetorically looking up at her surroundings. She was in some sort of cavern with some objects which looked like they should have been white but the mud on the floor had stained them so much that they now looked more like a dirty black. "Bones!" exclaimed Madelyn disgusted by the revolting sight. Madelyn got up onto her feet and walked over to the wall to inspect the carvings there. They seemed to be depicting two men fighting on a plain. "The War of the Slaves," whispered Madelyn, brushing the dust off the wall. "I remember father telling me about this but what is it doing down here?"

"Who are you?" asked a voice behind Madelyn. Madelyn almost jumped out of her skin with the suddenness of the voice. There behind her was a man with black soot scattered all over his face. "You first," said Madelyn.

"My name is Gelandov," replied the man.

"How long have you been down here Gelandov?" asked Madelyn.

"Longer than you could imagine," said Gelandov. "I was here ever since my dratted brother threw me into this abyss and left me to die. If I hadn't known how to fend for myself I would have joined the bones on the floor."

"And your brother is?" said Madelyn dreading the answer.

"His name was Galidion," said Gelandov.

"I need a way out of here," said Madelyn turning back towards the wall and frantically searching for any type of hidden door. Gelandov stood up and came over to Madelyn saying "Don't you think that if there is a way out that I would have found it by now?"

"Oh yeah, but you're not me," said Madelyn continuing to search the wall.

"Who are you may I ask?" said Gelandov looking intrigued.

"I'm not going to stay long so I don't need to bother telling you my name," said Madelyn, moving over to scan the back wall of the cavern. "I told you my name," said Gelandov, "Why don't you return the favour?"

"It's Princess Madelyn," replied Madelyn.

"The Princess," snarled Gelandov sounding angry. "Cameron's daughter! Oh I am so sorry." Madelyn was forced away from the wall as Gelandov picked her up off the floor and chucked her back down. Madelyn rolled next to the pool and when she looked up she saw her sword lying a few feet away from her. It must have slipped from her belt when she fell. "You're an enemy to our kind," said Gelandov, walking over and picking Madelyn's sword up off the floor. "What are you going on about?" asked Madelyn, afraid to get up because of what Gelandov might do with the sword. "The War of the Slaves," said Gelandov as if it was obvious. "It was because of what your father did in that war that made my brother send me down here."

"That was my father, not me," snapped Madelyn.

"Same thing isn't it?" said Gelandov leaning down with a creepy grin on his face.

"You're crazy," shouted Madelyn, trying to get back up off the floor but Gelandov knocked her back with a blow to the head. "Don't you dare move!" said Gelandov, turning away. As soon as Gelandov turned his back Madelyn jumped up and hit him on the back of the head and she watched with anger as he slumped to the floor. Madelyn quickly marched over to the back wall picking up her sword on the way and she started to scan the wall again. "Please Madelyn, I'm sorry," she heard a voice whimper. She turned around and saw Gelandov on the floor with tears flowing from his eyes. Madelyn made her way back to him while saying, "I'm not the enemy here."

"I know," said Gelandov, "but I am sorry to say that there is no way out. I have spent three years looking for one but I can't find it, we're doomed." 'Oh great' thought Madelyn 'I'm going to be stuck down a hole for the rest of my life.' "Okay," voiced Madelyn sitting on the cold stone floor of the cave.

Cold Blooded Murderer

Madelyn was struggling to get to sleep that night because of the thought that she was confined to this hell hole for the rest of her life. She heard soft and subtle footsteps next to her. It was probably just Gelandov getting a drink of water from the pool that Madelyn had fallen in when she first got here. Then she heard a more unusual sound. It was the sound of metal scraping against stone and then she heard a voice whisper. "I must do what has to be done," 'That's weird,' Madelyn thought to herself before opening her eyes. She saw a knife just inches from her face and it was Gelandov that held it. "I'm sorry," he said to Madelyn his voice trembling, "But I have to do this, for my brother."

"Gelandov," said Madelyn trying to reason with him, "Your brother tossed you down here without a second thought. Do you really think that if you kill me you will get some congratulations?"

"I am not doing it for congratulations," said Gelandov, with a tint of madness in his eyes "I am only doing this because it's right." Madelyn just had time to roll out of the way as Gelandov brought the knife down. It hit the stone floor where Madelyn had lay a moment before. "You don't have to do this Gelandov," said Madelyn.

"I do," said Gelandov, with another swipe of his knife, this time knocking Madelyn down to the ground. "Get up and do what your father would do and kill me," said Gelandov.

"No I won't, I'm not my father," said Madelyn.

"Such a shame," said Gelandov kneeling down and swiftly putting his knife against Madelyn's neck. Madelyn felt that soft cold metal against her neck and the soft slow sounds of hers and Gelandov breathing was the only thing that could be heard in that damp cave. "Gelandov," gulped Madelyn but she didn't get further than that as Gelandov brought the knife even closer to her. Just one more inch and that knife would decapitate her. She had to say the right thing or she would die. "Gelandov, I can help you," said Madelyn.

"No one can help me, especially not the daughter of the person who got me trapped down here in the first place," said Gelandov.

"What has my father got to do with the reason your brother threw you into this blasted abyss?" shouted Madelyn.

"There is something my brother wants, something your father possesses," said Gelandov, taking the knife away from Madelyn's throat by a few inches. "The throne," said Madelyn trying to sit up only to find the knife at her throat again. "I shouldn't be telling you this, my brother would kill me," said Gelandov.

"Your brother isn't here, he can't hurt you," stated Madelyn, gasping for breath.

"He's stronger than you think," said Gelandov.

"I know I've met him, but no one is as strong to reach you down here," said Madelyn gently taking the knife from Gelandov's hand. He didn't try to stop her and she could see that there was tears in his eyes. "Please tell me what you know."

"The king's heart has been broken," said Gelandov.

"What do you mean?" asked Madelyn. He didn't answer. Then Madelyn did something she didn't expect, she picked up the knife and put it against Gelandov's neck. "WHAT DO YOU MEAN?????" shouted Madelyn, spittle flying from her mouth. Gelandov just laughed and said, "You wouldn't dare stab me."

"Are you sure about that?" sneered Madelyn, stabbing Gelandov in the arm and listening in pleasure to the sound of him screaming in pain. Madelyn pulled the knife out and watched Gelandov writhing on the floor. "Are you ready to tell me what I want to know?" asked Madelyn. "Never," spat Gelandov.

"Very well," said Madelyn, brining the knife down once more, this time stabbing him in the shoulder. "No, please stop. I'll tell you what you want to know," said Gelandov.

"Good choice," said Madelyn her knife half way to stabbing him in the knee. "So what did you mean the king's heart is broken?"

"H-h-he, t-t-thinks you're dead," explained Gelandov, staring at the knife that was still clutched tightly in Madelyn's hand with an edgy expression. "You were the only thing that kept him fighting, without you he is nothing."

"How do I get out of here?" asked Madelyn.

"You can't," said Gelandov.

"I've had enough of your lies today so just tell me how do I get out here or do I have to stab you again?" asked Madelyn stroking the knife.

"I'm being serious you can't," said Gelandov.

What if he was right? What if there was no way out? What would she do then? "The king is going to die and there is nothing you can do to stop it," stated Gelandov. He then took that moment to reach for Madelyn's knife. She saw him coming so she threw the knife right across the cave and into the lake. Gelandov watched as the sharp point of the knife sank beneath the surface. Gelandov ran for the lake hoping to catch the knife before it went too deep. Madelyn stood up and kicked him in the back. He went tumbling to the ground and went skidding across the floor until he joined the knife in the lake. "If you won't help me then I will find a way out myself," said Madelyn, staring at the place where she had seen

Gelandov go below the water before walking over to inspect the back wall of the cave for any sort of escape route.

In about thirty seconds Madelyn found a little hole in the wall. She looked at the hole more closely and put a hand on the edge of the hole. A few rocks crumbled away and suddenly the hole was the size of a doorway. On the other side of the wall was a little round cavern with a worn rope ladder on the opposite wall. Madelyn walked over to it and started to climb. When she was about half way she felt something grab her leg, it was Gelandov. "Let me go," said Madelyn trying to kick him in the face.

"Never," he shouted, trying to take Madelyn's sword out of her belt.

"Oh no you don't," said Madelyn, slapping his hand away.

"You are the reason for my imprisonment and I am going to make you pay," said Gelandov. "Get off!" shouted Madelyn, lashing out with her foot again and this time it made contact with his face. Gelandov fell down and down and when he was just about ten feet off the floor he grabbed a rung off the ladder and started to climb back up. "Oh no you don't," said Madelyn, pulling out her sword and starting to cut the rope of the ladder. "No!" shouted Gelandov, starting to climb more rapidly, "Please I beg of you!"

"I can't let you back up Gelandov, you could try and kill me again," said Madelyn finishing cutting one side and turning to start on the other. "I promise I won't try and kill you, as soon as we're out we can go our separate ways."

"I'm sorry I can't take that risk," said Madelyn, taking one last slice at the rope. It snapped and the bottom half of the ladder fell to the floor with Gelandov tangled in the within it. As Madelyn reached the top of the ladder she heard Gelandov shout, "Madelyn!" but she ignored him and climbed up into the light.

Arriving in Lemuria

As he kept on heading through the plains, Richard barrelled past the many green scenes on the horse he had stolen from a farm owned by an elderly couple. Normally he wouldn't have stolen it but he needed to get to Lemuria and fast. He had told Madelyn that he would keep the king safe and that was exactly what he would do. Even though he'd agreed to go back and help the king he must admit that he had, many times, felt the urge to stay and help her, especially after he had seen Galidion setting off in pursuit. In the distance the highest tower of Lemuria appeared through the trees and Richard jumped emotionally for joy; he had made it. The guards at the city gate stopped Richard and he stepped down off the horse coming over to the guards. "What is your business here?" asked one of the guards.

"I have a message for the king," replied Richard.

"The king is in mourning, come back in about a week," said the guard.

"But this important," said Richard

"You don't get to decide that," said the guard, "Now be on your way." Richard gave out a sigh and turned around creating the impression that he was leaving, though as soon as the guards took their eyes off him he turned straight back around and ran past them and through the gate ignoring their shouts telling him to come back. Richard ran through the city market trying to get as far away from the guards, who were now pursuing him, as possible. He was almost caught once but he pushed a market stall over creating a barricade in the middle of the street and by the time the guards had managed to clamber over it he was already far away. Richard came to the castle gates and didn't stop when the guards told him too. He ran towards the throne room and just walked right through the throne room doors not paying any attention to the guards who stood on either side and startling the king. "Who are you? What are you doing here?" stuttered the king, looking as if he had just seen a ghost.

"I mean you no harm," said Richard, taking out his sword and setting it on the floor before taking a few steps back, "My name is Richard."

"Well Richard what do you want?" asked Cameron.

"I carry some news," explained Richard.

"I hope it's not bad because I have had enough bad news to last me a life time," said Cameron, sadly standing up and walking over to a portrait of Princess Madelyn which now had a black canvas hung over it. Richard almost felt compelled to tell Cameron that Madelyn was still alive, but he didn't want to give him false hope. She still had a lot of life threatening things to face before she came home. "I am afraid it is bad sir," said Richard.

"Then get it over with," said Cameron, not taking his eyes of the portrait.

"Galidion and his army are on their way to Lemuria and they are very well armed," said Richard, "I think they mean to kill you." The king's expression turned from one of sadness to one of anger. "Not if I kill them first," said Cameron, walking over to the throne room doors and swinging them open to find five guards standing there. "Get to the city walls and defend our perimeter," ordered Cameron.

"But sir," said one of the guards.

"Do as I say!" shouted Cameron and then all the guards ran off to the city walls. "Now you go," continued Cameron turning to Richard.

"I will not leave you while you are in danger," said Richard.

"Then make yourself useful and help defend the perimeter," said Cameron. Richard ran towards the city gates and climbed the wall to meet up with the guards. "What are you doing here intruder?" snapped one of the guards.

"I'm here under the king's orders," retorted Richard. "Galidion is on his way here and we need to be ready."

"Oh no! I remember the last time that he came in the War of the Slaves. It was a massacre. We lost many good soldiers including my brother," said one of the guards.

"I am very sorry for your loss," said Richard, "but isn't that a perfect enough reason to stand up to him, to insure that no one else shares the same fate."

"Yeah," struggled the guard.

Daylight

Madelyn felt her eyes sting as they adjusted to the light of the day, while scanning the surroundings. She was in the same pass between the mountains where she had been when she went into that cave. She had wasted an entire day maybe even more, she couldn't tell down in that cave, but she didn't care, she was so happy to feel the soft muddy earth beneath her fingertips. Then she thought about it; if she had come out close to the cave that could mean Galidion was also close by! No, he can't be because he had watched her fall down a one thousand foot drop, and he would have presumed her dead. "That means I can get the flower without any trouble," said Madelyn, voicing her thoughts out loud as she struggled to her feet. She was struggling to get her bearings, which way had she come from? It was a one out of two chance of choosing the correct path so she stumbled on down the path to her right. The sun seemed to be getting warmer, or was that just Madelyn. She stumbled to the floor, maybe she was wrong. Without Galidion following her the quest was still unbearable. Her heartbeat was fast and she couldn't stop thinking that she had made the wrong choice. She could have saved him. Gelandov was only human like her and humans could be saved. 'But what if they can't?' said a voice in her head, the voice of a woman. The voice sounded kind and gentle but her words were full of hate. 'What if the only solution is death?' And with those words, Madelyn drifted off to sleep.

The Far Lands

The next day Madelyn woke at the break of dawn and set off once more almost immediately stumbling into the Far Lands. She realised this was the place by the change of climate and scenery. Madelyn wiped the sweat off her brow as she stared at the deserted wilderness of The Far Lands. Sand was blowing in face and she brushed it out of her eyes. 'I knew The Far Lands were bad, but I didn't know they were this bad' Madelyn thought to herself.

The intense heat of the sun was almost unbearable to Madelyn as she trudged on through the sandy scene of the Far Lands. Her mind never strayed off the thought of her father as she continued to her journey's end. 'What would her father think when he heard the fake news of her death? Was he safe? Had Richard got there in time?' These were just a few thoughts that troubled Madelyn but if she was going to get through this she was going to have to push the thought of her father out of her mind. She had no idea where she was going and which way the cure lay, no matter which way she turned the sandy scene still looked the same. There were no distinguishing landmarks for her to keep track of the route she was taking but at least Galidion wasn't following her, which was something. Even without Galidion, Madelyn was struggling to continue the quest and she felt the sand spilling into her shoes. She knelt down and untied the laces of her leather shoes so she could empty them of the huge amount of sand which had somehow made its way in. As soon as she had emptied her shoes she put them back on and double tied the laces before continuing. And the whole day went like that; Madelyn kept on struggling through the sand dunes and constantly had to stop to empty her shoes of sand. Finally, night came and the sun went down but the temperature didn't. She decided to stop and rest for the night but with the high temperature Madelyn found that she couldn't get to sleep. As a result, she stayed awake thinking about all the people who had helped her to get as far as she was; Richard, John, Violet, Mary. There were so many kind people in the world but then there were some that weren't as amiable; Galidion and Gelandov, who had both tried to kill her in their own cruel ways. Why they were like this, Madelyn didn't know.

Sandstorm

Madelyn trudged on through the desolate Far Lands wondering how long she had been going for and more importantly, how long she still had to go. Dehydration clawed at her throat making her want to just lay down and die. Her vision started to blur from exhaustion which was caused by the humid air and she stumbled, getting a mouthful of sand. She couldn't believe how feeble she had become. Right now she would do anything to feel ice cold water on her parched lips. Then it dawned on her; what if the Black Leaf wasn't even in the Far Lands? What if Wilfred's books were wrong? What if it didn't even exist? She was going to die for nothing. Madelyn felt some grains of sand in her eyes. She brushed them away and looked up in the direction she was heading. Madelyn saw masses of sand being blown towards her - a sandstorm! "Oh no!" Madelyn whispered to herself, heading back in the direction she had come from. No matter how fast she ran the sandstorm kept getting closer. She couldn't outrun it. She felt the sand storm envelop her and she tumbled to the ground.

Madelyn felt a sting in her eyes as a result of the grains of sand that were piled on top of her. She felt her breath get heavier as she slowly started to suffocate from the sand that had buried her alive. Madelyn moved her hand to the side by an inch and felt the humid air envelop her soft skin. She felt sweat trickle down her palms but it was still better than death by suffocation. She had to get out.

Breathing was becoming harder by the second and she felt sand flow into her ears and start to impair her hearing. Madelyn sat up and felt the sand fall off her and with it a massive weight was lifted off her chest. She could finally breathe the open air and it felt so good to feel it against her skin once again. The sandstorm had hit her so hard burying her in seconds. She was afraid that if something like that was to happen again it would finish her off.

Madelyn struggled to her feet and then stumbled back down coughing so hard that it felt like something was living inside her clawing at her chest trying to dig its way out. Through the blur of the sand she could see a shimmer of hope on the horizon, something that could help her through this daring and deadly quest. It was a village! Madelyn metaphorically jumped for joy, she could do this, she knew she could. Madelyn crawled towards the village. As she got closer she heard the excited chatter of the villagers. They had seen something they hadn't seen in years, it was an injured and dishevelled girl making her way towards the village. Some people believed that it couldn't be possible, no-one could survive this far out in The Far Lands but here she was in the flesh smiling like she hadn't smiled in months.

The Last Leg

Feeling relieved by her night's sleep, and the hospitality shown to her in the village, Madelyn continued her quest. Her eyes were starting to sting as they adjusted to the light of the sun. Madelyn had been travelling for hours, or at least she thought she had, when she saw it. Growing in the desolate plains there it was! The whole reason she was here, the legendary Black Leaf. "I've made it," said Madelyn with relief, "I've actually made it."

Madelyn started to run towards the flower when she felt something grab her from behind. "I don't think so," said the voice of Galidion. Madelyn struggled to break free from Galidion's grasp but he just tightened his grip. Then Madelyn pulled her sword out of her belt and sliced it over her head. She heard a growl behind her and then Galidion's grip loosened. Madelyn turned around and saw a cut right across Galidion's face and he put his hand on it in the hope of stopping the flow of blood. "You rotten little girl," growled Galidion with rage.

"That is for all the pain you caused my father," said Madelyn. Galidion ran at Madelyn and dealt her a blow to the face. "OW!" screamed Madelyn. But before Madelyn could react fully, Galidion disarmed her. Once Galidion had the sword he thrust it into Madelyn's stomach. As Madelyn felt the immense pain of the sword stabbing into her, she knew this was it, this was how she was going to die. Galidion pulled the sword back and blood flowed staining Madelyn's clothes and she slumped to the floor. Galidion's laugh rang in Madelyn's brain causing her to have a headache. "So I have finally done it. I have made the lie that I told become the truth," said Galidion, standing over her as her vision started to blur.

Galidion ran off into the plains in the direction of Lemuria. Madelyn wouldn't give up, she might die but she was going to make sure that the cure got back to her servant first. Madelyn used her shoulders to turn on to her stomach and she started to crawl slowly towards the Black Leaf. She could feel sweat trickling down her brow from the intense heat of the sun. Her eyes started to droop and she had to use whatever strength she had left in her body to not succumb to the sleepiness of death. "Come on Madelyn," said Madelyn to herself, seeing how close she was to the flower, "You can make it." She stretched her hand towards the Black Leaf and she felt her hands curl around the stem. Then the pain in her stomach became almost unbearable as her hand let go of the cure and she succumbed to the sword wound.

<u>Waiting</u>

Richard felt the cool breeze against his forehead as he stared out at the kingdom. Madelyn should've been back by now, he really hoped nothing fatal had happened to her. The kingdom was in disarray, it felt like they were just waiting for their deaths. The king had organised to fight but even he knew that they could only hold out for a day, a week maybe, but eventually they would all die. Richard watched and waited knowing the inevitability of what was coming but he just wished that Cameron would stop risking more lives than was necessary.

There were a series of terrified screams coming from the city gate so Richard leant over the wall, as far as he dared, and saw the gruesome and horrible sight of a castle guard with an arrow protruding from his back. Richard sprinted down the stairs on the inside of the castle wall, pushed past the hundreds of onlookers who had gathered to get a closer look. Richard reached the man and knelt down next to him. "What happened?" whispered Richard. "They came too fast," croaked the man, "We could not withstand an attack of their calibre. They told us, to tell you, that a new king is coming and that Cameron had better run."

"We need to get you to the hospital," said Richard, as the guard keeled over his body rattling with coughs. "You're wasting your time," rattled the man, "You should be reinforcing the barrier around the city. They are coming."

"You're delirious," said Richard, "you need medical help."

"Can't you see?" said the man, getting increasingly angry, "You must get some men together and reinforce the wall." Richard didn't think this was necessary but to put the man at ease he set some men to guard the wall and then headed off with him to the castle hospital.

Madelyn eyes opened slowly and she saw Violet standing to her left. "Oh my goodness, don't say they got you to? It's one thing me dying but not my best friend as well," whispered Madelyn. "Madelyn," said Violet coming over and sitting next to Madelyn "You're not dead. I found you lying almost lifeless on the plains so I took you back and bandaged the wound. You should heal over time."

"I was so close Violet," said Madelyn, sounding pained by the thought of the flower in her grasp, "But I didn't make it to the cure."

"Oh, don't worry about that. I got the flower for you," said Violet, picking something up that lay next to Madelyn. It was the Black Leaf. "You got the cure," said Madelyn, with a sigh of relief, while gently taking it from Violet, "I need to get back." Madelyn swung her legs out of the bed and found that she was in Mary's living room.

Delivering the Cure

Madelyn burst through the door of Wilfred's Pills and Potions while shouting, "Wilfred!" Wilfred came out of the back, which is where Madelyn assumed the store room was, carrying a pile of about ten dusty old books that looked to Madelyn like they hadn't been touched in at least a century. He looked over to see who his customer was and when he saw Madelyn he dropped the books causing an explosion of dust which in turn caused Madelyn to have a coughing fit. Wilfred, who wasn't fazed at all by the dust, just stared at Madelyn with amazement. "Are you a ghost?" asked Wilfred.

"No I'm real," said Madelyn.

"But it can't be," exclaimed Wilfred.

"It's too long to explain, but Wilfred, I have got the plant. Now can you make the cure?" said Madelyn showing him the Black Leaf. Wilfred looked at it with a serious face and gently took it from the palm of Madelyn's hand. "Shouldn't take too long," said Wilfred, disappearing into the back of the shop.

Madelyn burst into the hospital with the wooden bowl, that held the cure to heal all wounds, and rushed over to where she had last seen her servant. He still lay there but this time he looked almost unrecognizable. There was a dark purple mark that outlined his left eye and Madelyn could see the sword wound was infected. "Please don't be too late. We can't be too late," Madelyn whispered to herself, putting the bowl on the side of the hospital bed. Madelyn got a wooden spoon and stirred the mixture in the bowl around. She forced the servant's mouth open and poured the cure down his throat. Then she gently set the bowl on the table next to the hospital bed and she waited for something to happen but nothing did.

Madelyn put her hand on her servant's forehead and felt his temperature and it was increasingly high. "Oh no, this can't be happening! I saved you. I got the cure. I can't be too late," whispered Madelyn. Still nothing happened and Madelyn felt the tears flow down her cheeks, she was too late. After all she had been through to get the cure, she had still been too late. "Madelyn," whispered a voice next to Madelyn and she looked up in surprise to see her servant lying there with his eyes wide open and a big smile on his face. "You're alive," said Madelyn stating the obvious, while crying tears of joy, "Oh my goodness, you're alive."

"Well, well, well so you actually managed to do it," said a voice behind Madelyn, "You managed to succeed where so many others failed."

"William," whispered Madelyn turning around to face the man who had pretended to be a friend to her father but all along she had known he was a traitor. "You should be dead," sighed William, "I should've known Galidion was too weak to finish the job."

"I know about the plan to attack Lemuria and I won't let you do it," said Madelyn.

"Do you really think that you, an eighteen-year-old girl can really defeat an army?" asked William laughing.

"I am not just any girl I am Madelyn, Princess of Lemuria." That just made William laugh even more. "Titles don't scare me. You are nothing! You couldn't even save your servant," he chortled. Madelyn looked behind her to see her servant gasping for breath as his face turned a sickly shade of green. "What's happening to him?" asked Madelyn, turning to William. "I administered a serum that counters the effects of the Black Leaf," said William, looking proud of himself. "You've killed him," whispered Madelyn.

"Oh no, he's alive, but only just. I will you two, to say good bye to each other," and at that William turned around and left the room. Madelyn ran towards the doors and swung them open. The corridor was empty with no sight of William. She would have to deal with him later. Madelyn turned around and ran back towards her servant just as he took his last breath and his body went rigid. Madelyn's servant was dead.

Friendly Advice

Richard made his way towards Cameron. He had to convince him to call off the attack. If he didn't hundreds of people, thousands maybe, would die and Richard could not let that happen. Cameron was in the meeting room going over the war plan one last time. "Sir may I have a word?" piped up Richard.

"One minute Richard," said Cameron, observing the map of the kingdom.

"This can't wait sir," said Richard. Cameron looked up and saw the deathly seriousness that was depicted on Richards face. Cameron gestured to the men to continue making plans while he let Richard lead him to the side of the room. "What is it?" snapped Cameron.

"You need to call off the attack," said Richard.

"No I won't," said Cameron.

"But can't you see, this is what he wants."

"You don't get to make the orders," said the king, sounding disgusted.

"I'm not ordering you," retorted Richard, "I'm offering you some friendly advice."

"Yes I know and I thank you, but we've got to end this," said Cameron, his mind made up. "This is about Madelyn isn't it?" said Richard, knowing full well that Madelyn was alive and had returned to the castle but the king didn't know that. He didn't intend to let him know anytime soon either. He was absolutely positive that the truth would finish him off. "He killed her," said Cameron with a pained voice.

"But if you kill him, would that make you any better?" asked Richard, grabbing the king's arm so that he had no other choice but to look at Richard. No one would ever dare touch the king because there was a chance that you would be on the spot, but desperate times required desperate measures. "I don't care what that makes me," said Cameron, breaking away from Richard's grasp, "Just that her death is avenged."

He had to tell him, he had to, Cameron would want to know that his precious daughter was alive but just because he might want to know it didn't mean telling him was the right thing to do. The huge battle of emotions raged on inside Richards's body pushing him to breaking point. He didn't know what to do. What could he do? In the end, Richard decided to keep quiet for now because if he told him, Lemuria's last hope would be gone.

Castle Ablaze

Madelyn struggled down the corridor as everyone ran the other way. She had to elbow some of them so she didn't end up getting washed away in the sea of terrified people. They were all so scared about the attack from Galidion and his army, that was imminent, that they didn't pay the slightest bit of attention to the fact that the princess they had all presumed dead had returned. She had to find her father before William...

The wall to her right exploded and she was blasted into the wall opposite as a shower of rubble rained down on her. The attack! The attack had started. Black dust obscured her view but she still managed to see that most of the people who had been in the corridor at the time hadn't made it. It was horrific. Madelyn hadn't ever seen so many dead bodies in one place at one time. There was no other damage to be seen apart from the huge gaping hole in the wall where the explosion had first occurred. Madelyn had a long strand of hair in front of her right eye so she pushed it behind her ear and then it was clear to see that there was dull red glow coming from amongst the rubble. The castle was on fire! Madelyn pushed a piece of rock off her leg where it had landed when the wall exploded. She had never seen the castle in such chaos and destruction. Everyone was running around with evidence of some sort of damage inflicted upon them - probably cause by the explosion. Soot covered the floor so no matter where Madelyn went she either had her hands or feet covered in it. Madelyn wanted to help these people but she knew that her father was her first priority. Then she looked at the faces that were either stained with soot or tears and then thought, why should she go after her father who was just one man who hadn't cared about her much anyway, when she could save thousands? Her father was a strong man; he could defend himself. Madelyn had to save the city. The choice had come down to: save thousands of innocents or one tyrannical man. Her decision was made.

Cameron and Richard walked through a door to a balcony overlooking the main courtyard. Richard saw the small snowflakes fall slowly down to the ground and then melt in the fire that now burned in the courtyard. "I told you! I told you this would happen and you didn't listen," said Richard, with bitterness in his voice watching the fires rage on.

"A few mere peasants," said Cameron, staring across the city. Just in their line of sight they could see Galidion and his men storming the many buildings that housed the people of Lemuria. 'Where's Madelyn' thought Richard, scanning the city for that long scarlet hair that in the last few weeks he had come to know so well, 'Where is she?'

While Richard looked for Madelyn, Cameron looked at Galidion's army with anger in his eyes, like a fire that could never be extinguished. "They must die. All of them must die," decided Cameron. "You can't do that," said Richard, stopping looking for Madelyn and looking at the king. "I'm the king," said Cameron, turning to face Richard, "So I think you'll find that I can."

Cameron got ready to leave the balcony and go back into the castle when Richard lashed out with his hand, grabbed Cameron and shoved him into the wall. Cameron unsheathed his sword but as soon as he had it in his hand Richard kicked it and it went flying off the balcony. Richard grabbed the front of Cameron's jacket and once he had hold of it he pinned Cameron against the wall. "GUAR..." Richard put a hand over Cameron mouth and shushed him whispering;

"You know this is for the best." Cameron tried to say something but his voice was muffled because of Richard's hand clasped over his mouth. "Do you promise that you're not going to shout for the guards?" Cameron gave a terrified nod and Richard let go of his mouth and freed him from the wall. "You're working for Galidion," assumed Cameron.

"No I'm not."

"Then why did you attack me then?" asked the king confused.

"Because as much as I would like to tear Galidion limb from limb for what he did to Madelyn, I would not risk thousands of people to do so," said Richard.

"You didn't know Madelyn. She would want this," said Cameron.

"I did know Madelyn and she wouldn't want this," said Richard, kneeling next to the king. He knew there was no diminishing the cruelty in his heart but he could try, "I'm not asking you to agree with me, I'm ordering you. If you go ahead with this suicide mission I will stop you."

"Then do it," said Cameron, tears filling his eyes. Richard couldn't bring himself to do it, it was either the whole city or the king but he couldn't bring himself to do it. Madelyn wouldn't want that. 'Since when was this about what Madelyn would want,' asked a voice at the back of his head. 'It has always been about her' argued another voice. "I thought so," said Cameron getting back up and walking back into the castle

"I can't move my legs," screamed one of the citizens grabbing the lower half of her body. She was a petite woman with beautiful grey hair that only came down to her shoulders. The woman had scars patterned across her face and tear stained cheeks. "You have to try," said Madelyn, who had knelt down in front of her trying to help the woman to her feet, "No one is getting left behind."

"It's already too late for me," whispered the elderly woman. Madelyn looked left and right down the corridor, trying to spot anyone who would help her with this woman. When she saw that nobody was moving, she picked up the woman and started walking down the corridors. More walls started to crumble as the city capitulated to the scale of the attack. Madelyn was devastated by the sight of her home in ruins. She just hoped that her father was all right. She couldn't help thinking that this wall her fault. If she hadn't set out on the quest would this have happened? Those questions Madelyn would never know the answer to. The only thing she could do was save the city. She rushed down some stairs, the heels of her shoes echoing on the cracked stone. She was weighed down by the bulk of the woman slung across her shoulder and she could feel the dampness from her tears. They were so close to the entrance. Madelyn felt like the whole world was in slow-motion as rock fell to the floor and the front door became shrouded in dust. 'Come on you can make it' echoed a voice in Madelyn's head, which she didn't recognize, but Madelyn had a feeling that it was her mother communicating to her from beyond the veil that separated the land of the living from the world of the dead. 'Yes it's me dear' continued the voice, 'Your time will come but you need to keep moving.' Madelyn stumbled right, through the door, before a rock fall closed the entrance to the castle and Madelyn along with all the survivors were trapped on the outside.

Enemy on both sides

Galidion stood on a hill overlooking the battle. His men had managed to take over most of the city, the only area they hadn't taken over was the castle. It was almost over. Galidion knew that. Soon the throne would be his but he just had to make sure of it. He walked over to his right hand man and said, "We need to put them in a predicament that they can't get out of."

"What are you suggesting sir?" asked the man.

"Take a group of men and attack the castle from the back. Let's see how Cameron deals with an enemy on both sides," said Galidion.

"Yes sir," said the man rushing off. Galidion smiled with glee as he turned back to the onslaught of the city of Lemuria. He really wished he had kept Madelyn alive just so he could see her face as she stared at her city that she had lived in for so many years being razed to the ground. Galidion then decided that after all Cameron had done, he could not be left to the mercy of his men. Galidion was about to enter the battle.

A selection of Galidion's finest men lay just below the back of the castle. There were two staircases leading up to the castle from this side and the men had decided to divide themselves and take a staircase each. "Remember," said one of the men, "Galidion wants Cameron alive."

"Why though?" protested one of the men, "It would be easy to just kill him."

"No! Orders are orders."

"I don't care, Galidion doesn't scare me."

"Then by all means go ahead and kill Cameron, but I wouldn't like to be in your shoes when Galidion finds out." The man who had just spoken then turned to the rest of the men and said, "Remember, the castle of Lemuria is one of the most guarded places in the entire kingdom. That is because it is owned by a king who despises all. Eighteen years ago, Galidion devised a plan to rid the kingdom of that treacherous king and finally on this glorious day the plan has been put into action. Galidion has entrusted us, his most faithful soldiers, to put an end to it once and for all, to ensure that today is the day Cameron dies."

"Yes sir!" shouted the men, their voices echoing all the way up to the darkened room which was abandoned apart from Richard and Cameron. "They are coming sir," said Richard, looking through a narrow slit in the wall that was at the back of the room and observed the band of men. "I know Richard," said Cameron looking at him, "They are about to storm the throne room from behind and all they think they're going to find here is me so leave and you will be safe."

"I'm not leaving," said Richard. Cameron nodded to the side of the room and two guards stepped out of the darkness. One grabbed Richard's left arm and one grabbed his right. "What are you doing sir!" shouted Richard, struggling against the will of the guards.

"It's for your own good," said Cameron, before saying to the guards to throw him into the lake. "You traitor," shouted Richard, as he was dragged from the throne room. As the doors to the throne slammed shut, Cameron slumped into a sitting position on the throne and whispered to himself, "That was the hardest decision I have ever had to make."

Outside the throne room Richard was still struggling with the guards. "Listen to me," he screamed, "The kings in danger."

"We know," said one of the guards, as they dragged Richard onto one of the many castle balconies. The balcony overlooked the glistening lake that lay just outside the city wall. "Then why don't you do something about it?" said Richard, backing away from the guards until he was bumped up against the small wall. "Because he brought this upon himself," whispered the guard, who had spoken before. That didn't sound good. "What do you mean?" enquired Richard. The guard leant in so close that Richard could feel his slow breaths against his ear and said, "The king isn't who you think he is." Richard felt the man put a hand on his chest, "Now just relax." The hand pushed and Richard once again hit the wall but instead of stopping him from falling this time he went right over the edge and tumbled down towards the lake.

Trapped on the Outside

"No, No, No!" screamed Madelyn, pounding her fist on the rock which had replaced the entrance to the castle, "I need to get back in there."

"Princess Madelyn," said a stern voice behind her. Madelyn turned and saw the voice belonged to the woman she had carried out of the castle. "I think you need to explain," the woman continued, "How can you be alive?"

"You want to do this now?" asked Madelyn sharply, "Can't you see that we are at war?"

"Yes I can and it is because of that, that I am not ready to just accept that our princess is back. For all we know you could be an imposter."

"Well I'm not," said Madelyn, looking for a weak spot in the rock.

"Can you prove it," said the woman nonchalantly.

"Jenny," said Madelyn walking over to her, "Jenny Oswald, my friend? Remember when we were six? Every Sunday we used to go down to the lake and skip stones. You used to always get annoyed because I could throw further than you." Jenny looked as if she was about to cry before whispering, "It is you."

"Yes it is, now it's time to go to war," said Madelyn.

Battle at Hells Rift

The new captain of the guard, Lucas, led his group of soldiers into the courtyard and stared at the raging fires in glee. "Okay ready men," he said, turning around to see his soldier's eyes. They were all too young for this. Too young to die, but that was like saying everyone else wasn't. He had to encourage them. Make them believe that this was possible. All he could bring himself to do was hold his sword high above his head and shout, "For Lemuria, may no one break these walls." That was all they needed. They shouted for Lemuria before charging into the battle field.

Cameron had instructed them that they needed to focus on Galidion; once Galidion was dead it would all be over. Cameron would feel like a giant weight had been lifted off his chest knowing his daughter had been avenged. This was almost over. They turned a corner onto Emlenton Avenue and then they saw him. He had finally shown his face in the battle, the man himself, Galidion. "Wait," said Lucas, putting his hand out to stop one of his men from charging him. He ordered all of them back into the alley they had just come from. "Why did you stop me?" said the man, "I could've stopped him."

"Running in blindly like that! Yeah, I would have liked to see you try," said Lucas mockingly, "You need to learn, soldier, that running in like that can sometimes get you killed. We need a strategy."

"We haven't got enough time," protested one of the soldiers and the raised voices of the other soldiers murmured in agreement. "Then make time," said Lucas, peering around the corner once again to see Galidion stab someone in the head. Lucas watched in disgust but then he realised that this scene held a good strategy. "He's alone," announced Lucas, "Oh this is brilliant! His biggest mistake yet."

"So we outnumber him," said one of the men, coming over to look at Galidion as well. "Surround him," said Lucas, gesturing to the rickety ladder that was next to them and led up to the roof of the building that they were stood against. "Will do sir," said the man, saluting to Lucas. "Hey boys, we've got a plan." Lucas watched as half of the men followed the solider up to the roof. The rest of them went down another alley so they could get behind Galidion, while Lucas had left himself the hardest job of all; distracting Galidion.

"Oi mister!" shouted Lucas, stepping into Emlenton Avenue, hoping that it would get his attention and it worked. "Oh and who are you?" said Galidion staring at him.

"My name is Lucas. I am a soldier working under the command of our king; Cameron. He wants me to tell you that you are not welcome here," said Lucas.

"Oh, and where is the man himself?" shouted Galidion, scanning the rooftops as if he was up there. Lucas saw Galidion's eyes were almost where the men lay in wait. Lucas couldn't let him see them otherwise they would have failed the king. They would've failed to fulfil the duty they had been set. "He's not here," said Lucas, his plan didn't work. Galidion's eyes were almost there. "And why is that?" said Galidion.

"He's scared of you," said Lucas. He knew that wasn't true but he would do anything to stop Galidion from looking at those rooftops. "Oh really?"

"Yeah," said Lucas nodding.

"No, I meant did you really think that that would distract me from your friends sneaking across the rooftops?" He'd seen them! "Or your friends that are trying to sneak behind me using the alleyways." 'We're done for!' thought Lucas.

"I must admit. It was a valiant try but now I'm going to have to kill you," said Galidion. The moment he unsheathed his sword the five men who had taken to the alleyways burst into the street.

Dead

Lucas stared down at the bloodied corpses of his men. Galidion had killed them all like a demon from hell. A demon that didn't care who lived or died as long as he got what he wanted. What Lucas didn't understand, and made him begin to suspect if Galidion was human at all, was the fact that he had killed ten men! Ten very powerful men and he didn't have a scratch on him. This man had killed his friends, his comrades, his brothers in arms. This man was the reason that their princess was dead. Who was next? Lucas had to do something. It had come down to this. He was going to be the hero he had always wanted to be. He was going to show the king that he could save the city. He could end the Battle of Hells Rift.

Lucas stood up. Galidion turned around and noticed Lucas on his feet. "Some people never learn," said Galidion. Lucas had nothing to say to this man. He didn't want his apologies or him begging for mercy. He wanted blood. Lucas swung his sword but Galidion dodged and then grabbed the sword and yanked it out of Lucas's hand. Once he had it in his hand he used the hilt to knock Lucas off his feet. Then pointed the sword at his neck. "I just killed your entire banner of knights. I don't want to have to kill you to," said Galidion. "Don't think for one second that you can convince me that you actually care for these people," said Lucas.

"I do," said Galidion, "It isn't their fault." The sword started to inch away from Lucas's neck. "What isn't their fault?" asked Lucas.

"The king is controlling them. He is a tyrant. He has been lying to the city for years," said Galidion. Lucas looked in Galidion's eyes and saw a hint of tears and his eyes seemed to sting from a painful memory. Why did Galidion hate Cameron so much? "I want to save them," said Galidion.

"Save them from what?" asked Lucas.

"From the king," shouted Galidion.

"What did the king ever do to you?" asked Lucas.

"He took something from me that was mine,"

"The throne," whispered Lucas, "It never belonged to you."

"Father promised it to me," said Galidion, "because I was the oldest naturally it was me that was meant to take the throne. It was the right thing for the constitution. My brother always had it in for me. He wouldn't let me have the throne so he got me excluded from the city and I have lived ever since in the rotting wilderness." Galidion was Cameron's brother! It couldn't be! Galidion must be trying to fabricate a story so Lucas would trust him but it wouldn't work. Lucas lashed out with his foot and it came into contact with Galidion's face. In the moment of confusion, Galidion got up and ran back towards the castle. "The king won't save you now, he is broken," said Galidion's voice from behind Lucas. He didn't listen, he just kept running. He reached the castle and the first person he saw was the king. "Where are your men?" asked Cameron.

"They're dead," said Lucas panting for breath.

On the Losing Side

Cameron stood in his daughter's room. This was all for her. He had lost all these people for her. That is how much he loved her but he feared he hadn't said it enough. She probably died thinking that he didn't care. The whole castle shook, knocking precious ornaments off Madelyn's dressing table. Cameron looked at them with a sad expression as they smashed on the floor. It was over, they were all going to die. He should've listened to Richard. He should have called the war off. Maybe it wasn't too late - this had to end.

Madelyn looked through the gap of the ajar door of her room watching her father stare out of the window like a statue. A man deprived of love and loyalty, this couldn't go on. "Madelyn," whispered a voice next to her. She turned around and saw Richard beckoning towards her at the end of the corridor. She walked over to him. "Galidion's almost won, it's almost over," said Richard.

"No its not, I won't give in without a fight," said Madelyn, trying to walk past Richard but he put a hand out to stop her. "I won't let you risk your life on another suicide mission again," said Richard.

"This man has destroyed my home. Murdered my people! He won't get away with it," growled Madelyn. "Then let me come with you," said Richard. Madelyn stared into Richard's eyes. This was going to be dangerous. She couldn't drag him into it but how many times had he saved her life on the quest? He could defend himself. "Come on then," said Madelyn, leading him down the corridor. Two men ran toward them. Madelyn pulled out her sword and sliced at the guy on the left and he fell to the ground, blood spraying from his cheek. Without thinking she turned to the other man and stabbed him in the chest. "Since when did a girl like you learn to do a thing like that?" asked Richard, looking scared.

"I don't know, it just seemed natural," said Madelyn, shrugging her shoulders before continuing down the corridor. "Stop there," said another man from behind them. As quick as lightning, Madelyn pulled a small knife out of her pocket, turned around and threw it at the man. Richard watched in horror as it embedded in his skin and he fell to the floor. The quest had changed Madelyn. She was no longer the innocent little girl who wouldn't dare kill a soul. She was now a battle hardened warrior who was blinded by rage and would do anything to save the people she loved. That was the Madelyn she had become and it scared Richard. This rage could lead her to do something that in her later life she would regret. Madelyn saw he fear in his eyes. "Don't look too scared," said Madelyn, "Just because I know how to throw a knife."

"You've changed," whispered Richard.

"Of course I've changed," said Madelyn, "did you think that I would watch my whole city be razed to the ground and not do anything about it? Someone has to do something. Even if it calls for drastic changes."

"Oh this is drastic all right," whispered Richard, as he followed Madelyn once again down

the corridor.

They turned a corner and went through a small archway which led onto a spiralling

staircase. It was a very thin staircase, so thin that Madelyn had to keep her arms at her side. As they neared the bottom of the stairs Madelyn saw a guard stood staring right at them. Madelyn managed to turn her head just enough to see there was another guard stopping them from going back up.

"On my signal," Madelyn whispered to Richard. She waited a few minutes before shouting at the top of her lungs, "NOW!!" Richard just managed to turn around in the narrow stair way and he engaged in battle with the person behind him while Madelyn went for the man at the bottom of the stairs. In just a few moments the guards lay dead their blood staining the stone steps. "We need to keep going," said Madelyn, going through the archway at the bottom of the stairs. "No Madelyn. I can't come with you," said Richard.

"Why?" asked Madelyn turning around to face him.

"This war won't be won by a person who just runs in blindly killing everything in her

path," said Richard.

"What are you suggesting we do?" asked Madelyn.

"We have to think about the source of the problem," explained Richard. "These men are

here under Galidion's orders so if we find him and apprehend him then the war will be over."

"Apprehending him won't help. We need to kill him," said Madelyn with distaste in her voice. Richard grabbed her arm and said, "We need to talk."

"There's no time," said Madelyn.

"Madelyn, what the hell is wrong with you?" said Richard, "The last time we saw each other you wouldn't kill anyone! What's got into you?"

"Someone has to die and it won't be my father," said Madelyn.

"Madelyn, there must be some other way," protested Richard.

"There isn't," said Madelyn, walking down the corridor. Richard felt rough hands grab him from behind. He was just about to shout out for Madelyn when a hand shot out to cover his mouth. "Be quiet and embrace oblivion," whispered a voice behind Richard. Richard felt metal digging into his skin and then he fell to the ground motionless.

Imprisonment

"This seems to be happening to you a lot lately."

Those were the first words that Richard heard when he woke up in the dingy cell in the castle dungeons. Right in front of him, sat on a rickety wooden stool, was Galidion. "What are you doing here?" asked Richard.

"Oh haven't you heard? I own the castle now. In just a few hours it is going to be made official and I will be the new king of Lemuria," said Galidion.

"Cameron would never allow that," said Richard.

Galidion stood up. "You see Richard, Cameron doesn't have a choice," he said, circling Richard. "You will never win, someone will stop you," said Richard.

"You mean that little brat who calls herself a princess," said Galidion.

"How dare you say that," shouted Richard, lashing out with his foot. Galidion jumped back and stared at Richard with an amused smile.

"Nice try," said Galidion, kicking back and sending Richard, along with the chair he was tied to, crashing to the floor. Richard wheezed as all the breath was knocked out of him. "You'll never learn will you?" said Galidion, with a smirk of satisfaction as he watched Richard struggle with the rope that bound him to the chair. Galidion unsheathed the knife that hung at his belt while whispering, "I'm so sorry Richard but you gave me no choice." Galidion brought his knife down.

"Sir," shouted a voice from outside the cell. Galidion's knife stopped inches away from Richards face and he heard a grunt of annoyance emitting from Galidion.

"What?" snapped Galidion, turning to face the man. "We are under attack! The king's men are fighting back," said the man. Galidion looked at Richard, who was still lying on the floor, and said, "I will deal with you later." Galidion went to sheath his knife but unawares drops it to the floor before following the man out. Richard couldn't believe it! Galidion had been stupid enough to actually drop a method of escape right at his feet. Richard wriggled his fingers, trying to inch them further towards the knife - but it was just out of reach. "Come on, come on," said Richard, trying to stretch his hand just that little bit further. The chair wobbled, though with one final push the knife was in his hand. Once he had it in his grasp he brought it round to the back of the chair and sliced the rope in two. He was free! Relishing the feeling of having his hands free once more Richard made his way towards the cell door and to his surprise found it open. He stepped out into the corridor and headed towards salvation.

The Loyalty of Friends

Madelyn fought like a machine that had been programmed to kill anything in its way. For a few short seconds she was indestructible, that was, until she saw the state of the castle. Fires burnt everywhere and it had lost one of its towers. "It's bad, isn't it," said Violet, appearing at her shoulder. "It's horrible," sobbed Madelyn.

"That's one more reason to stop it and that's why we will stop it," Violet reassured Madelyn.

"Then let's get started," said Madelyn, rushing over the courtyard to the house that used to belong to John. Violet followed her. As Madelyn expected, the Johns family were found cowering behind the table. John's widow Isobel had her arms protectively around her two daughters, Gabriella and Stacy. Madelyn tried her best not to look at them in the eye. She hadn't seen them since John… No she couldn't think about that. "Hi Isobel," said Madelyn trying to sound brave for the children's sake.

"What's going on?" whimpered Gabriella. Her and Stacy were only five and six years old respectively so they hadn't been in the War of the Slaves whereas their mother Isobel had. Madelyn pulled Isobel aside. "You need to get them out of the city," whispered Madelyn, once she was sure they were out of earshot of the children, "I don't think we are going to survive this."

"But where would we go?" asked Isobel.

"There is a small town called Little Leaf. It's only a five-minute walk. I will try and come for you when all this is over."

"What if you don't come for us?" asked Isobel. Madelyn was about to answer when she heard a big explosion followed by a series of terrified screams. "Let's not worry about that," said Madelyn, ushering John's family towards the door. When they reached it Isobel turned around and grabbed Madelyn's arm. "Please come with us," begged Isobel.

"I can't," said Madelyn, "I need to find my father."

"But you'll die if you do," said Isobel.

"Then die I shall, but I must find my father first," said Madelyn, watching Isobel, Gabriella and Stacy being swept away by the crowd of citizens that were evacuating the city. "We're going to survive this," said Violet trying to reassure herself more than Madelyn.

"You will at least," said Madelyn, staring at Violet with a distant expression, "Get out of the city, don't look back, just run."

"What? No! I'm staying here with you," said Violet.

"That's an order," growled Madelyn.

"Then I refuse," said Violet bravely.

"You don't know what you're getting into," said Madelyn her lip quivering.

"Look, if you die, then I die with you," said Violet, raising her voice and waving her arms about like a demented lunatic. It was dangerous but Madelyn had to admit she liked the company. "Then let's get going," said Madelyn, leading Violet towards the door to find a solider standing in the doorway with his sword drawn. "Ah we've found you," he said, with a look of wry amusement.

"Get back," shouted Madelyn, grabbing Violet's arm and yanking her back as the sword dug into the wooden doorframe.

"Don't do this," said Madelyn, putting her hands up in a sign of surrender, "We don't have to fight."

"And why is that?" asked the man.

"Because Hells Rift should be a kingdom of peace," explained Madelyn.

"Do you really believe that?" said the man with a discreet chortle.

"Of course I do," said Madelyn, "War isn't the answer." The man let out a short burst of laughter before bringing his fist up in a swift uppercut that knocked Madelyn to the far wall. The man pulled out a knife. Madelyn stared at it with wide eyes. She had almost died at blade point before but luckily had survived. This time she might not be so lucky. The man threw the knife. Madelyn closed her eyes as the knife got increasingly closer. Then she heard the knife digging into skin but felt no pain. That could only mean one thing. Madelyn opened her eyes to find Violet just inches to her left, she was on her knees and there was a knife imbedded in her stomach. Violet had saved her life. Madelyn didn't say anything but just rushed over to Violet's side. "The wounds not too bad," said Madelyn, "I have to pull the knife out. This might hurt."

"Madelyn," Violet uttered almost inaudibly. Madelyn looked up to find her face deathly pale. "There are more important things for you to worry about than my health," continued Violet, "Leave me."

"W-we can ... I-I can help you," stammered Madelyn.

" We need to face the truth," said Violet, tumbling back into Madelyn's arms, "It's been good though hasn't it."

"Yeah it has," said Madelyn, a smile appearing through the tears as she watched the last bit of life drain from Violet's face.

Confrontation

Madelyn stared down at the lifeless body of her former friend Violet. Her eyes used to hold so much life but now they were filled with nothing but blackness. Madelyn couldn't help but think that it was all her fault. She had refused to kill that man and while doing so she had committed an act of weakness which Violet had paid for with her life. "This had gone on for too long," whispered Madelyn, her heart filled with anger. She knew where Galidion would be heading and she was determined to stop him from getting there. This was going to end, today. She pulled her eyes away from Violet's body and headed towards the throne room.

Madelyn stormed into the throne room and saw Galidion and Cameron at the far end in the middle of a heated argument. "Galidion!" shouted Madelyn. The throne room bestowed none of its former glory. The narrow slits in the walls had become gaping holes exposing the throne room to the open air. Madelyn made her way towards the two people who had played a big part in her life having to step over a dozen piles of rocks which had fallen from the ceiling. The first thing she had noticed when she entered the throne room was her portrait which had a black canvas strung across it. Galidion had created all these lies and caused so much pain for her father and for what? The throne? Surely he wanted more than that. Cameron and Galidion turned around both with a look of shock on their faces. "Madelyn," whispered Cameron, in disbelief that his daughter was actually alive. "Oh why can't you just stay dead?" said Galidion, his expression turning to one of rage.

"Because I have something worth living for," said Madelyn, drawing her sword while continuing to make her way towards him.

"Well it doesn't matter, I will enjoy killing you again," said Galidion, slicing his sword through the air. Madelyn dodged. "You are blinded by rage Galidion," said Madelyn, getting so close that their noses were almost touching. "You fail to see the bigger picture, you're just pathetic."

"Aaaagggggghhhhhh," screamed Galidion, swiping his sword once again, this time Madelyn blocked it. "There is someone in the world that is better than you, who was always better than you and that person is me," taunted Madelyn. This time Galidion delivered a blow so powerful that it knocked Madelyn off her feet. "Don't provoke him Madelyn, he'll kill you," said Cameron pleadingly.

"I don't care," growled Madelyn, slamming her sword down at Galidion and he blocked it but his whole body shuddered. Madelyn looked at him with a look of pure hatred, "Violets dead because of him."

"I am sorry about your friend," said Galidion, in a voice that almost made Madelyn almost believe him, "But her death was for a good cause."

"What cause could be so great that it drives you to murder hundreds of innocent people?" shouted Madelyn.

"Don't even attempt to understand," retorted Galidion.

"You're mad," shouted Madelyn, dodging Galidion's sword once more.

"If you really think you are better than me then prove it," said Galidion, holding his word out in front of him. "Gladly," said Madelyn tightening her grip on her sword.

Breaking of the Peace Treaty

Madelyn swiped her sword at Galidion in the hope of distracting him from the determination to murder her father. Galidion blocked it and delivered a blow of his own. This time it hit home by slicing through her soft skin and making blood pour from her cheek like a waterfall. Cameron stared in disbelief at the mutilated wound that Galidion had inflicted upon his daughter. "You indomitable pest," snarled Galidion.

"Is it my fighting skill or your lack of one?" taunted Madelyn

"Aaaggggggghhhhhh," screamed Galidion, bringing his sword down with extreme force. Madelyn managed to bring her sword up to stop it from hitting her in the face but the sheer weight of the blow was enough to knock her off her feet and onto the floor. Madelyn wished she hadn't teased him now because Galidion burned with nothing but fury and rage, shown by the clear madness in his eyes.

Madelyn took a quick glance behind her father, hoping that he would help her but for once in his lifetime he looked unable to do anything even for his daughter's sake. Madelyn had just looked back towards Galidion when she saw the sharp point of his sword plummeting towards her. She skid backwards, on her backside, across the hard stone floor as the sword came in contact with ground. Sparks flew from the sword and singed Madelyn's scarlet hair. "Leave my daughter alone," whimpered Cameron, from behind Madelyn.

"What did you say old man?" said Galidion, turning his back to Madelyn so he could face Cameron. If anytime was the time to strike it was now, it had to be. Galidion grabbed the king's chin menacingly and looked at him with a big grin on his face because he knew he was completely in control. There was nothing anyone could do to stop him. Cameron wanted to say something brave but in the end he just gave out a small terrified squeak. "Oh, is little Cameron scared," snarled Galidion, "I'll show you what real fear is." Madelyn saw a flash of silver making its way towards Cameron. She ran towards Galidion while screaming, "Noooooooo." Madelyn pulled her sword out, without Galidion noticing, and dug it right into his back. Galidion stopped short and his sword clanged as it hit the floor just inches from Cameron's feet. "That was for my father," shouted Madelyn, pulling her sword out of Galidion's back and then jabbing it back in again. "And that was for my servant," added Madelyn.

Cameron watched in disbelief as blood from Galidion's back splattered on Madelyn's cheek mixing with hers, creating a look of pure rage. Madelyn didn't know when she had realised it, but her father was right. Kindness wasn't the answer like she had originally thought. Some people deserved to die, just like Galidion. Every time Madelyn pulled her sword out and dug it back in again she felt like she was getting revenge for everybody she had lost: John, Violet and even her servant. Galidion dropped to his knees and Madelyn dug the sword in once more for good measure before watching him fall to the ground dead. "It's over, he's really dead," said Cameron, looking at the body to make sure he was actually dead. "Yeah it's over father," said Madelyn, resting her hand on his shoulder, "Lemuria can finally go back to a city of peace." A smile flickered on Cameron's stern face and he said, "You did well my daughter." Madelyn was shocked. This was the first time in her life that Cameron had ever complimented her. Cameron opened his mouth to say something else but nothing came out except blood. "What the?" said Madelyn, at her father. "Father what's wrong?" Cameron coughed and it shook his entire body as more blood stained the floor of the throne room. That was when she saw the crimson tip of a bloodied sword poking out from Cameron's abdomen and she knew that her father was about to meet his premature end. She didn't want to accept it but deep down in her heart she knew it was inevitable. The sword slid out of his body and he stumbled backwards onto the floor revealing the sight of Sir William of Greenmont holding his sword up victoriously. The same sword he had used to stab the king with, only moments ago. Madelyn could see that the sword was dripping with his blood. William looked worse than when Madelyn had last seen him. Sweat stuck his long black hair to his head and he had suffered major cuts and bruises from the battle. Not waiting around to see Madelyn's reaction William fled for the doors of the throne room.

Madelyn took one glance at the close to death body of her father before shouting, "GUARDS!" The guards tried to intercept William but he knocked them down as he barrelled passed. Madelyn stared into Cameron's bloodshot and fatigued eyes. "Madelyn I am so proud of you," whispered Cameron, while caressing Madelyn's cheek gently.

"Don't you go saying last words to me," ordered Madelyn, taking a closer look at the sword wound. it was worse than she had anticipated and she had to stifle a sob. "It's alright," said Cameron, taking Madelyn's hand and pressing it against his chest, "Be brave."

"But you can't die," said Madelyn, a tear rolling down her cheek.

"My time has come," said Cameron, accepting his fate, "But yours is only just beginning." "I can't take that much responsibility," said Madelyn.

"I'm sorry," said Cameron, in a hoarse voice, "But before I go, there is something you need to know about Galidion." There was a pause as Cameron took a deep breath that shook his entire body, "He's your uncle."

"What?" asked Madelyn, but he didn't answer. His eyes were glazed and he wasn't moving. "No, No, No!" screamed Madelyn, slapping Cameron's face as if she was trying to swat a fly. There was still so much she needed to ask him. Galidion couldn't be her uncle! How could her father be a brother to that monster? So many questions but she was sure about one thing, her father wasn't going to move ever again. Madelyn stretched out two fingers and with great care closed his eye lids.

With Cameron dead that left Lemuria without a king and because she was the rightful heir to the throne that responsibility immediately fell to Madelyn. Madelyn rose off the floor and got ready to fulfil her duty.

In Mourning

Madelyn entered the dark and cold throne room and made her way to the centre where there lay a coffin. It had been a whole week since the passing of her father, Cameron and Madelyn had mourned him ever since. Soon the coffin would be transported to the tombs below and then the last remaining piece of her father would be gone.

Madelyn stroked the coffin and felt a tear roll down her cheek. "Don't you dare go saying last words on me," said a voice in her head. Then she realised it wasn't a voice, it was a memory. There was nothing she could do to stop the flashbacks. The blood splattered on the floor and Cameron's body went limp in her arms. So many memories, so many things she wanted to forget. The tears falling down her cheek, her voice screaming, "Noooooooo." She had to fight this, she couldn't fulfil her duty to the city if she was like this. She couldn't believe that her father was gone. There was so much she still had to tell him, that she couldn't tell him now that he's gone.

Guards came into the room ready to take the coffin and Madelyn's eyes filled with tears. She felt a hand rest softly on her shoulder and she turned around and buried her head in Richards's chest, feeling the tears flow down her cheeks. "I know, I know," whispered Richard, rubbing Madelyn's back gently. Richard then took Madelyn's hand and they then walked out of the throne room holding hands.

A few days later Madelyn was looking out of her bedroom window when Richard came in. "They're ready for you,"

"I don't think I can do this," said Madelyn, her memory set on her father's dying words: "He's your uncle." That wasn't possible. Cameron and Galidion had despised each other for as long as she could remember. They couldn't have possibly been related. Her father would want her to do this. He would want her to inherit the throne and strike fear in the hearts of their enemies, her enemies. She couldn't possibly be strong enough to take that responsibility. She didn't know how he had handled it. If her father had done it then she could as well. She just hoped there was such thing as heaven so her father could gaze down upon her, his precious little girl, and see the woman she was about to become. "You have to," encouraged Richard, wrapping his arm around her waist and pulling her closer, "It's your destiny."

"Yeah," she let out a sigh, "Sorry it's just all a bit too sudden," apologised Madelyn, forcing herself to look up into Richards's eyes. 'Since when did they look so beautiful' Madelyn thought. "You don't have to be sorry," said Richard, lacing his fingers with hers, "Just remember that you will never be alone. There will always be people there to help you."

"I won't forget," said Madelyn, a smile flickering on her face.

"Then that's alright then," said Richard, returning the smile before leaning down and matching his lips with hers. In that moment Madelyn lost track of time but she didn't care. She knew today was a special day but she couldn't remember why. All she knew was the feel of Richards lips against hers. She heard the clanging sound of a bell in the distance. 'What's that for?' wondered Madelyn. 'Does it matter?' said another voice, at the back of her head. She knew she had forgotten something but Richards's lips tasted so sweet and then she remembered. "The coronation," said Madelyn, pulling away from Richard, "We've got to go."

Madelyn and Richard sprinted down the corridors towards the throne room where thirty years previously her father had faced the exact same situation that Madelyn was to face today. They reached the doors of the throne room and Madelyn took a deep breath. If she chose to go through those doors she would come out a completely different person. She parted the doors and timidly entered the room. She walked down the aisles between the hundreds of people sitting on seats, her eyes flickering from each one like a scared mouse. These people expected her to be their ruler but if they found out how much of a coward she was they might be having second thoughts.

In her peripheral vision Madelyn noticed Richard sit down on a seat in the back row, his hands shaking with nervous tension which didn't help. Inch by inch the throne got closer; the throne that used to belong to her father, the one that would now belong to her. Madelyn finally reached it and sat down staring at Wilfred who had been appointed the job of crowning her. "We are all gathered here today to witness the start of a new era. The era of Queen Madelyn." There was an outburst of screams and people shouting, most of them shouting, "Madelyn!" Madelyn's eyes scanned the crowd looking for Richard and found him with a big smile on his face. They believed in her, he believed in her, she could do this. She saw the Arch Bishop of Lemuria walk towards the throne with a purple velvet cushion and on it lay the crown. This was it, this was the time. In a few seconds she would be the ruler of Lemuria, she couldn't do this, yes she could, she must.

Wilfred took the crown off the cushion, with great care, and started to take it towards Madelyn. The crown was pretty basic made out of silver instead of gold but the sapphire that adorned it was the most beautiful thing that Madelyn had ever seen. It was nothing like Cameron's, seen as though that was broken during the Siege of Lemuria, which is what people now called the outrageous battle in which the king's life had been broken. "I crown you, Madelyn, Queen of Lemuria," said Wilfred's voice and then Madelyn felt the crown getting being placed on her head. "Long live the Queen."

The voices echoed around the room. She had finally done it; she had become Queen. She was sat in the same position her father had been all those years ago and now she was ready to face whatever journey lay ahead.